CW01498879

Blood ink

C. J. Davies

Cover Design by CJD Design
Edited by Dr Ashley Lister PhD

© Copyright 2020 Colin Davies

'Raven and Skull" used with kind permission. © Copyright 2016 Ashley Lister

The right of Colin Davies to be identified as author of this work has been asserted by him in accordance with the Copyright, Designs and Patents Act 1988.

All rights reserved.

No reproduction, copy or transmission of this publication including any part of the text, design or artwork may be made without written permission. No paragraph of this publication may be reproduced, copied or transmitted save with the written permission or in accordance with the provisions of the Copyright Act 1956 (as amended).

Published by Word Rabbit book (via Amazon KDP)
ISBN-13: 979-865107931-5

Acknowledgements

This has been a fun book to write; however, I would have never finished it without the support and understanding of my partner Heather Brennan. For this, I am truly thankful, and I love her and our son Stephen very much.

I also send love and thanks to my editor Ashley Lister. A fantastic novelist in his own right, the encouragement and time he gives me are invaluable. You will also find within these pages a reference to *Raven and Skull*. It comes from a book called *Raven and Skull (ISBN 978-1910720530)* written by Ashley. He has allowed me to use the name and setting, which is really kind of him. I highly recommend you pick up a copy.

There are also massive thanks going out to my friends Mick Arthur, Iayn Dobsyn, Tony McMullan, Steve Brown, Charlie Hart, Matthew Bartlett, Jason Brashill and Dylan Freeman. Between them, they have listened to me waffle on, read first drafts and encourage me. They are a source of energy that helps every day.

With so much love, I thank my mum, Moyra Davies. She gave me a passion for books and is always encouraging.

I must also thank my reading team. I find it very useful to have a few people to read through my work before publication. They're not looking for errors, nor are they trying to find ways to improve the text. Their role is one of quality check. They read it to gauge the entertainment factor of the book. With their feedback, I know this book you are about to read is as enjoyable as it can be. So, thank you to: Simon Jay, Heather Freeman, Tony McMullan, Charlie Hart and George Stephenson.

Finally, I wish to thank you, the reader. Without you, us writers would just have heads full of stories and no one to tell them to. So thank you for reading, and I hope you enjoy it.

It is here that I would also like to point out that the other writers named within these pages are characters and not actually other writers. Just in case anyone thinks I'm being mean by not thanking them.

D.F.G.M
Always

"It's a modern-day first-person horror."

The office was dark with just a single Luxo lamp sitting on a huge wooden desk, directed at an empty green leather captain's office chair. Hidden in shadows behind the thick smoke of her cigar, the producer waited silently. It was exactly as Simon had described; intimidating, disorienting and more than a little bit erotic – for those with darker tastes.

James was ready.

Everything Simon had told him so far had led to this point. The advice he gave on the letter, *"More punch. Tell her, you know how good this idea is..."*, his suggestions on the story, *"put something of yourself into it..."*, even the timing of when to send the approach, *"Never post anything on a Friday..."*

Now he was taking a seat opposite one of the most powerful people in Hollywood. Although it was only recently that he found this out. Until Simon had suggested trying to make contact, James had never heard of her.

His research confirmed what Simon had been saying. The most powerful people in the industry, the biggest names, the most successful movies, they have all come through this office; they have all struck a deal with Ms Nikita. Now it was his turn to impress. His chance to pitch a story that could change his life and turn him into one of the most sought-after writers in the business, just like Josh Wotten, who had also sat in this chair.

James was a bit of a fanboy of Josh ever since his hugely popular TV series back in the 90s *Teenage Vampires: Eat Wood*. The sharp pop culture references and solid witty scripts spoke to James in a way no other show had ever done before. He started to notice the writers in the credits of films and TV shows. Studying the dialogue and admiring how scenes flowed together. It was Josh Wotten that had opened his mind to becoming a writer and, even though his hero had fallen from grace, James still held his talents in very high regard. If Ms Nikita could help him achieve half of what Josh had, James knew his career would be legendary.

A bright orange glow crackled as the producer drew in hard on her fat Cuban. The subsequent exhale fired a jet of cigar smoke clear across the desk and into James's face. The smell reminded him of his Uncle Kevin; before he was put away for abusing James's brother. After that, he only ever saw him once, and then he stank of disinfectant. Simon never forgave Uncle Kevin, but he did use his contact book to great effect and become a kick-ass agent. Silver linings.

Ms Nikita placed her stogie in the rather realistic skull ashtray on her desk, cleared her throat with a phlegm-filled hack, and then spoke with a soft south Kansas calming tone which took James by surprise.

"So, my pretty." Her leather chair creaked as she leaned back, "pitch me your story."

Broken Window
By
James Kilmore

C. J. Davies

Growing up on *the council estate*, had some very interesting aspects. One was the social bubble. As a child, I played within the confines of the local area, and so didn't really see much else of different social class other than on the TV. The other was the steady stream of temporary friends from the two children's homes on the corners of Chelwood Close and Cuckmere Way.

I lived in the ground floor flat of one of the grey-faced, three storey buildings that had been scattered across the hillside just after the war. My bedroom window had an unobstructed vista of the pathway that leads off the Close, which gave me a great view of the children's home up the hill. The one opposite, this was boarded by bushes and trees.

One night all the children were suddenly removed from the home. Me and my brother were woken up by engine noise and lights. Our parents were in bed so it must have been very late. We looked out of the window to see the kids being marched up the bank and into a minibus. Once they left, three removal trucks pulled up. We sat silent as they took furniture and boxes, loaded them on the trucks and drove off. There was a woman shouting at a couple of police officers. I recognised her from home. A tall thin woman often dressed in jeans and a white shirt. Her loose permed brown hair bounced in the street lights as she was forced in the back of a police car.

The next day the home was still, though the net curtain still gave it a sense of being inhabited, Nobody spoke about what had happened, we all just accepted they were gone, like other friends that had 'moved on'.

After a few weeks, we started playing in the gardens,

teasing each other with ghost stories and throwing stones at the windows. Many got broken, but always quickly replaced, probably by the invisible caretaker. It was this instant fixing that gave me the idea of how we could get into the house.

The trouble with broken windows is twofold. One, it makes a lot of noise, so once a smash occurs, running must ensue and two, broken glass is sharp and can cut you so climbing through can be dangerous. However, what I noticed was, once they were replaced the glass it would take a few days for the putty to dry out and go hard.

I was playing with one of the kids from the other children's home that was still operating. I never knew his real name, we just called him Smurf. He was about a year older than me but much more worldly-wise. The authorities had taken him from a family of Romanies. This was his fifth home. He'd run away from all the others.

"I'm born with travelling blood, no one can keep me in one place."

We were in the garden of the abandoned children's home. The high hedges enclosed the area away from prying eyes, which was perfect for getting up to mischief. It also had an unusual effect on the sound. The estate was built on top of the South Downs, so even though there wasn't a lot of traffic noise, there was quite a bit of nature. Birds, wind and trees all make a sound. Most of the time you just filter it out and walk around oblivious to it. However, once you remove the sound and deaden it down, you notice. It heightens your senses, putting you on edge. It didn't matter how many times we played there, the feeling of excitement was always amplified.

I walked over to the kitchen window next to the back door.

"We broke this window yesterday."

"I know," said Smurf, lighting a cigarette, "They're always fixed the next day."

"Watch." I dug my finger into the putty, which was still soft.

"So."

I continued to scrape away at the putty until it was no longer stuck to the window glass or the frame. I was left holding a small ball of blue, tacky dough.

"Great," he said, "I have plasticine at home."

I smiled and squashed the ball on to the middle of the glass then, using the putty as a makeshift handle, pulled the glass clean out of the frame.

"Mother shit balls." Smurf dropped his fag and ran over to me. "You little genius."

Laughing he put his hand through the opening and undid the latch of the window. The frame swung open. Without hesitation, Smurf climbed through the opening and into the kitchen.

A muffled voice echoed out of the window, "There's a key in the back door."

A rattle and click later I was in the kitchen. Everything had been stripped. There were bare floorboards; gas pipes sticking out of the floor where the cooker once lived; capped off water pipes. Whoever emptied this place knew what they were doing. There wasn't so much as a cabinet left. Even the light bulb was gone. The doors, however, were still in place.

We walked through to the front of the house where we thought the dining room would be. Again, the room was bare, the gas fire, table, chairs, carpet, all gone. The only thing remaining here was a black and white photo of five children in the back garden. Two girls and three boys, all different ages; they looked like they were going to a fancy-dress party all wearing old clothes, but not from the same time period.

We moved through to the living room. Fireless, carpetless, bare and void of anything, it was hard to imagine that there used to be 12 children and two adults living here. The hall had the same bare floorboards with wooden stairs leading up to the first floor. On the window ledge at the bottom of the stairs was a cream coloured telephone. Smurf picked up the receiver.

"Dead!"

As he replaced the handset the phone bell gave a solitary *ding.* The pair of us stopped, my heart raced. The seconds felt like minutes as we stood like statues, then, simultaneously, we both started to laugh. I walked up the stairs followed by Smurf.

It was darker up there. The doors to the rooms were open, but there were wooden shutters on the windows. For the first time, I felt an atmosphere. The empty rooms downstairs were just that, empty rooms. These felt, I don't know, it was like we were explorers entering a freshly opened tomb. I entered what I assumed to be one of the bedrooms. As I passed the door I noticed a bolt on the outside. *"They used to lock them in?"* I thought.

I turned to talk to Smurf about it. He stood silent at the top of the stair holding his finger to his lips to tell me to be quiet. It was then I heard the sound from downstairs; heavy footsteps and a scraping sound, like stone on wood, like something being dragged. Smurf furiously waved his hand to tell me to hide.

I looked around. There was a cupboard built into the alcove so I moved as quickly and quietly as I could and climbed inside with the dust and spiders. There was a gap under the door so I lay down to peek through. Being towards the back of the cupboard restricted my view. The footstep got louder as whoever it was climbed the stairs, the thump of whatever was being dragged made my heart skip as it hit each step.

Suddenly the sound stopped. My heart beat so hard I thought the sound would give me away. My breath was so shallow and quick I felt dizzy. Then came the scream. For all the maturity I thought he had, for all the bravado that came from his gypsy blood when terror struck, his scream was that of a child in absolute terror.

A sound like someone smacking a meat cleaver into a cabbage silenced him. I could hear movement, not walking, more shuffling, small movements; the sort of repositioning you do when lifting something big. The heavy boots I heard climbing the stairs entered the room. Behind the footsteps, the sound dragging on the floor wasn't stone on wood: it was metal. A huge single-headed axe with a wet-looking edge scraped the floorboards. The noise made me want to scream.

I put my hands across my mouth.

They came closer to the cupboard but stopped in the middle of the room. My mind raced with ideas. I could burst through the doors shouting at the top of my voice and make my escape before they knew what was happening. Or I could slowly sneak out of the door and crawl unnoticed. Or wait for the door to be opened and...

There are certain sounds you never forget. Like the sound of the car door being closed the last time you saw your father; or the crackling radio on the hip of the policewoman as she tried to explain to your mother why it was the last time you saw your father; or the dead thump when a bloodied body is dropped on a wooden floor head-first.

This sound was followed by Smurf staring at me from under the door. His eyes were lifeless. Blood was splattered across his face. The angle of his limbs was wrong, all twisted. There were no plans in my head now: no way I could think of to get out of this alive.

Staring at the crumpled body of my friend, I didn't notice his murderer walk over to the cupboard. I jumped as the head of the axe landed hard on the floor in front of me. This sharp noise was followed by a gentler tap as the wooden handle rested against my hiding place.

I urinated.

The killer then pulled the axe away, dragging it across the floor. I saw the killer's hand as they stooped down to grab Smurf's foot. Then, as if they were dragging a sack of potatoes in each hand, left the room and headed downstairs. I heard three very distinct sounds moving down the wooden steps; the killer's boots; the metal head of the axe and Smurf's head.

I lay perfectly still in a puddle of piss until there were no more sounds.

I pushed the door open and tried to stand but it was pointless. Fear had taken the bones and muscles from my legs. I fell forward onto my hands and knees and vomited. With tears in my eyes, puke on my shirt and wet pants I dragged myself to the door.

Out in the hallway, the light of the afternoon sun exploded up the stairs. This gave me the impetus I needed to run. No waiting for the killer to return, no thought that they might just be waiting downstairs to hit me in the chest with the axe as I tried to run past. All I wanted to do was get home.

Down the stairs and out through the back door. I didn't scream. I just ran. No one was in as I got back to the flat. I stripped and washed my clothes in the bath before putting them in the washing basket. In my bedroom, I closed the curtains and sat on my bed. I wanted to find my mum and just cuddle into her, I wanted to phone the police but what was I going to say?

"Me and my friend broke into a house where he was killed by a mysterious person and *yes, that gypsy kid who keeps running away from the children's home is missing, again!"*

They wouldn't give a toss, and all I would do is alert the killer to my presence. I made a pact with myself to never tell another living soul about this, ever.

*****

A few years had passed. Me, mum and my brother had moved to the town centre. I was in my last year of high school and had been invited to a Halloween party at Mike Burnage's house. This was quite a surprise as being a bit of a loner, I wasn't invited to many places. My best friend Dylan had requested I go. I had a knack for remembering ghost stories and he thought it would be a good place to share some of them without looking weird.

I dressed as a vampire. I liked the supernatural stuff, ghosts, werewolves, zombies, all the stuff that wasn't real. Serial Killers were not high on my favourite scares list. I still had nightmares but kept the fear in by filling my head with this horror nonsense.

It was a typical teenage party. The hard boys were getting off with the popular girls. Everyone cheered when a beer was opened. The music was loud yet nobody was dancing. I went to junior school with the lad playing the music. His parents had bought him a couple of turntables as he wanted to be a part of this new DJ-thing that was on the rise with all the new hip-hop and dance music coming out of the States.

As the evening wore on the numbers dropped, soon there was just me, Dylan, Mike, a girl called Tracy, her friend Lucy and the DJ Chris. Some tunes played softly in the background and Dylan suggested I tell a couple of spooky tales. This had the desired effect of getting Tracy to cuddle into Mike whilst Dylan got to play the big hero with Lucy. Just after I had finished the tale of the *'Queen's Park Grey Lady'* Chris asked the group if anyone had ever done a *Ouija Board*. The girls look scared.

"No it's fun," Chris tried to reassure them. "Mike, have you got Scrabble?"

"I thought you wanted to contact the dead, not play word games with them."

"No, dickhead." Chris used his hands to mimic a board. "We can make one with it. We put the letters in a circle and use an upside-down glass."

Mike stood up and fetched the board game from the shelf. "Wine?"

"Yes, you do," laughed Dylan. "A fucking lot as well."

"The glass." Mike flicked his middle finger at Dylan. "Will a wine glass do?"

Chris took the board game and started to set up on the floor, "Yeah, that's perfect."

He placed the board face down and sorted the letters so that the entire alphabet was in a circle. In the centre, he placed the wine glass so that the base was up.

"Right, now everybody needs to place the index finger of your right hand on the glass."

We did as he asked. There was some nervous

laughter and name-calling. Mike and Dylan were being all manly to prove they weren't scared, yet their eyes told a different story. Chris had the air of a scientist conducting an experiment. I was just doing it for a laugh. The dead weren't scary. It was the living that frightened me.

Chris asked the question in a strange deep voice, "Is there anybody there?"

Everyone went silent. Chris asked again, "Is there anybody there?"

Just then, Dylan farted. The nervous tension was released in an explosion of laughter. It took at least 10 minutes for us all to compose ourselves again. We all resumed the position.

"Is there anybody there?"

The glass twitched, then smoothly slid across the board coming to a stop by the 'C'. Before anyone could speak it was off again, 'O', then again 'L'

"OK, " I said, "who's pushing it?"

It kept moving 'I', 'N'

"Why has it spelt out your name Col?" Mike said

"I don't know?"

Chris joined in, "I don't know either, that's only 6 points."

The glass kept moving, letter after letter, 'Remember'.

My heart was beating fast, "This isn't funny guys."

'M'. Then, with a violent scrape, 'E'. The glass started to move round and round, faster and faster. A jolt, like static, pushed our hands off the vessel. The glass flew off the board narrowly missing Lucy's head before smashing into the wall. The girls screamed, Chris, Mike and Dylan yelled. I sat in silence.

Mike threw a letter at me. "*Colin, remember me. What the fuck man?*"

I couldn't speak. The others all raced around, shouting at each other about cleaning up; scaring the girls; and mum's best crystal. I just sat there. Mike called me many names, all of which referred to mental health but none of it mattered. Without any control, I spoke softly.

"Smurf?"

"SMURF?" Mike was furious, "You need locking up!"

That was the point when I realised he was blaming me for this. I stood up, holding back my tears. I fixed eye contact with our host.

"Trust me," there was a cold reality in my voice, "there is no way in the world I would do that. What I want to know is, who fucking pushed it?"

Something about me made everyone very aware that I wasn't messing about. Someone here either knew something about my past or had just luckily stumbled on a random phrase that hit the mark. Either way, I was now in a very unstable frame of mind.

"Fuck all of you!"

I left.

*****

I was restless, feeling a need to return. I moved away from the South Coast nearly 30 years ago. Pushing all the memories far down, so far that I didn't even talk to my brother any more, nor did I make the 300 plus mile trip to visit my mother now her and dad were back together again under the same stone. But I felt restless, and I needed to go back.

I parked the car at the bottom of Cuckmere Way and walked up the hill. It was the same route I used to take home from school. I reached the corner of the Close and looked further up at the old children's home. It was now a private house. I turned my attention to the building on my left. From the outside, it looked no different. I approached the gate that lead to the front door.

The open front door.

Curiosity got the better of me. I opened the gate and approached the entrance. As I walked through the gate the sound changed around me. It was that long-forgotten deadening of nature.

It was like being 11 again.

I slowly walked towards the door calling out to see if anyone was there. I could see the hallway had a carpet, as did the stairs. It looked like this was also a private dwelling. I peered inside and called, "Is there anybody there?"

For some reason, I felt compelled to step inside. Like flicking channels on a TV my mind switched between the lovely decorated home before me and images of the bare heartless building from my youth. I walked through the living room and into the dining room.

"Hello? Is there anybody there?"

In the middle of the oak table that now furnished the room was a black and white photo. I picked it up to have a look. Confusion filled my mind, this was the photo from all those years ago, I recognised the five kids at the front dressed in different period costumes only, this wasn't possible, there were now loads of other children, all dressed from different time periods. And there, just behind the boy from the original, was Smurf.

I swallowed deep to hold back the vomit that wanted

to escape. I turned it over to see if there was anything written on the back, then flipped it over to the image again. Nothing made sense, it was impossible but then, oh then I saw it, and fear gripped me. Stood at the back of all the children, was me. Everything around me disappeared. The room, the furniture, the carpet, the only thing I could see was me standing at the back of a photograph of children from over 30 years ago.

Then she spoke.

"Did you think I'd let you go?"

I turned around. Standing there was a tall thin woman wearing jeans and a loose-fitting white shirt. The curls of her soft permed brown hair bounced against her pale sharp-featured face. I looked down at her feet. Those boots, oh my God those boots.

I urinated.

Looking up I saw the axe coming down...

"It's a modern-day first-person horror."
(reprise)

C. J. Davies

The office became silent as James uttered his final words. The number of thoughts going through his head astounded him. There were only three possible outcomes; she loved it, she hated or it left her cold. Two of which James had convinced himself would be the result of this meeting before he even entered the room.

But now he was allowing himself to consider the notion that she loved it and this day was the start of a revered career. Less than a second into this fantasy and the long years of self doubt didn't so much as creep back, but burst through the walls of confidence like the *Kool-aid man*. He was fighting the urge to reach for his smartphone and apply for a job handing out chicken that had been judged to be 'not a witch' after a spell on the ducking stool of the deep fat fryers.

The air across the desk glowed a deep orange as Ms Nikita took in a deep smoke-filled breath. She let the pale wisps spill from her mouth. James could almost make out her face in the darkness as the cigar smoke danced across her features. He felt his throat go dry.

"You hate it, don't you?" his voice started to break with emotion but he just couldn't take the tension any longer, "Oh God, you hate it. I'm rubbish at this. I'm better off as a chicken finder general. Sorry to have wasted..."

Ms Nikita's soft Kansas notes harden slightly. "Will you shut the fuck up?" She opened a drawer in her desk and produced a ream of paper. To James, the pile looked about five hundred pages thick. "I think it has potential. Couple of changes here and there maybe. I mean, does it have to be set in England?"

"Umm, no."

"That's good. Very good. It's hard working with folks that are too married to their work. Mr Kilmore..."

"Please, call me James. I'm not comfortable with the whole 'Mr' thing."

"Ok, *James* that will be the last time you ever interrupt me."

James felt sick. Like the centre of his torso had just developed a black hole and all his internal organs were being sucked into it.

"I'm so sor..."

"I'll ignore it this time. Anyway, as I was saying. I would like you on my team. I have this *little ol'* contract here. I think you'll find it's fair." She pushed the ream of paper across the desk, "Son, I'm gonna make you famous."

"It's asking the question; how much do you trust apps?"

This was the most exciting day of Samantha's life to date. She was such a movie geek that, if you had told her this morning she would be having a video meeting with the one and only Ms Nikita, she would have called it a *complete fantasy*. Very few people even knew Ms Nikita existed, even though she was behind some of the biggest box office successes in the history of film.

Her productions had broken some of the biggest stars from actors to directors. More writers had been plucked from obscurity and given a platform to shine and share their art through projects backed by Ms Nikita than any other producer. Even the other big producers owed a debt to this enigmatic powerhouse, and yet she chose to hide her name from the spotlight

But Samantha knew her. Or, at least, she knew of her before the phone rang that morning with an invite to a face to face. When she hung up the call her mind was in denial. The small office in her humble terraced house was covered in posters. They were posters for films that Ms Nikita had a hand in, yet there wasn't a single written credit for her on any of any of them. It was an obscure article by a little-known journalist that revealed this movie mogul's name. Samantha wanted to know more so she phoned the magazine only to find the reporter had died in a car accident just a month after writing the piece.

As she looked out of the window at a quiet Morecambe road, this almost forgotten seaside town in the UK felt like it was a billion miles away from the studios of Hollywood. Yet, moments from now, Samantha would be pitching her story to a person she perceived as the most powerful woman in the world.

It didn't matter how many times she moved it, or how tiny the adjustments she made: the keyboard just didn't fall into a comfortable position for Samantha. She knew there would hardly be any typing done in a voice and video chat, but this was the woman that helped *Quinlan Targtain* make his seminal work *Dam Dog Fiction.* Everything had to be perfect. From the correct choice of books on the shelf behind her to the angle of the monitor. The keyboard wasn't feeling comfortable and had to be adjusted. The speakers, tapered in to achieve perfect audio. Even the package that had arrived 25 minutes after the phone call, which Ms Nikita's assistant told her to *keep nearby but not open yet,* had to be in just the right spot.

The echoing sound that accompanied the video chat notification of someone requesting connection *pinged* through the speakers. Samantha drew in a deep breath while feeling both sick and excited at the same time. The mouse pointer hovered on the *join call* button. Even though it was comparatively small, it felt like it filled the entire screen. A slight twitch of the index finger and Samantha's monitor was filled with the dark red of Ms Nikita's smiling lips. The contrast of this dark colour and the sharpness of her black eyeliner was intensified by the porcelain paleness of her skin. Ms Nikita's face, framed by flowing locks of raven black hair, appeared disarmingly innocent. Her soft Kansas twang made Samantha feel relaxed.

"Well hello there Sammy," she said. "May I call you Sammy?"

"Ummm, yes, yes. Many people do. Thank you."

"Don't worry my little pretty one, at this distance I can't bites ya."

Samantha felt a calmness wash over her as she laughed. Ms Nikita leaned on her desk using her elbow as support for the large cigar she held in her left hand. Smoke shrouded her face as she sucked the flame from her gold and jewel-encrusted *Zippo* through the tobacco.

"Please," she said using the cigar as a way of beckoning Samantha, "don't wait for me to catch fire. Tell me your story."

C. J. Davies

MinzPyz
by
Samantha Broadman

"It's an algorithm that means you can never buy the wrong Christmas gift ever again."
Buster Peterson *(CEO MinzPyz™)*

This Christmas was going to be perfect. Jennie had booked the ideal location to spend some alone time with Joe: something they never got in their busy day-to-day. It was a picturesque villa up in the hills of Spain overlooking Torrox about 50k west of Malaga on the Costa del Sol. Since the weather got all fucked up by industry, it had become the must-go-to place for a snowy Christmas break.

The dinner of *LabTurkey™* with all the trimmings was to be delivered by drone precisely at 3 pm, just in time to watch the big festive special that everyone was talking about. Even though Jennie had no idea what the big festive special was, they were going to watch it.

She had even convinced Joe to install *MinzPyz™* on his PWN: his Personal Wearable Network. Jennie had done the same, so it was fair. They had done this back in January, as a new year's resolution. Once Jennie had secured *Casa Del Sol, Torrox,* the villa's address was entered as the point of delivery. Nothing was left to chance. At 10:30am, just after breakfast, the *MinzPyz™ Surpryz™* would deliver the perfect gift for each of them.

This was going to be the most perfect Christmas ever!

"Basically what Minz Pyz is doing is watching everything you do on social media. It trends your life and calculates what you want, not what you need."
Barbara Winwood (Editor in Chief, *That's my Tech, Ezine.*)

The couple arrived shortly before 11 am on Christmas eve. Their *Automicab*™ pulled up to the gates at the top of a long driveway that ran down to the villa. The white walls, built when the seasons were normal, hardly did their job as they tried hard to keep the building cool in the searing heat of the modern summer. Currently, the colour was acting as a coordinated icing that blended with the snow-covered ground and thick piles of drift that had settled in the terracotta roof tiles. To the right of the property, the summer pool was now their personal ice rink, and the gardens had the perfect incline to be a rather good nursery slope.

As instructed by the booking-in screen, Jennie and Joe made their way around the back via a small set of steps that took them up past the ice rink. Taking in the view they smiled at each other like a pair of excited school kids.

Catching Jennie by surprise Joe suddenly darted forward to instigate a race. Though, as soon as he turned to get under the roof of the terrace, he deliberately slipped, letting Jennie win. They laughed as Joe brushed the snow off himself. Two keys and two doors later they were inside.

The place was as perfect as Jennie had imagined. A small galley kitchen was immediately to the left. Cooking wasn't high on their priorities, but breakfast needed to be poured and wine needed to be chilled. The kitchen was divided from the main living area by a marble serving counter. The villa management system had been alerted to their pending arrival as the *Automicab*™ reached the bottom of the hill when they were ten minutes down the road. So, the wood burner was now roaring, the coffee pot was fresh, and the faux-fur rug was newly vacuumed. The doors were shut to keep out the cold, but neither of the couple locked them.

They simply dropped their bags and gave in to the passion that wanted to test that rug.

> *"One of the reasons we buy gifts is to show the other person we care. What the gift is doesn't matter. It's the fact they thought about it. So what if it's not exactly what you wanted?"*
> **Dr Mary Hutchingson** *(Head of human research at Sussex University)*

After Jennie had taken great glee from being very loud in her exaggerated orgasm, much to Joe's delight, she had a quick check around the place. To the front of the villa, the old porch had been glazed to form a viewing room. It was the ideal place to drink breakfast while gazing out across the beautiful vistas of the snow-covered Spanish hills. There were only two weeks before the heat returned for a four-month season. If this Christmas went as well as she had planned, she thought they might come back to top-up their tans before the fields started burning again.

Joe was still lying on the rug with that stupid grin on his face as Jennie passed through.

To her left, there were two bedrooms. One had a couple of single beds with the bathroom just outside the door. The other was the one she was interested in. A double bed and *en suite,* though with just the two of them, the whole building was their own private love shack.

She returned to the stupefied Joe who was still lying on the rug in the main living area.

"Come on," she said pulling on her black *Sex in the Snow*™ knickers which came with a heated pad to *keep you warm both front and back.* "Let's go and play in the snow. Then we can come back and warm up all over again."

Joe smiled broadly and rushed to get dressed. The pair raced outside and started throwing snow at each other before collaborating on a couple of anatomically correct(ish) snow people. The snow woman had carved genitals and moulded breasts. The Snowman was bestowed with two carrots. One for the nose, the other stuck in with some force by Jennie. The pair laughed in a way only kids and couples in the giddy stage of passionate love do. Jennie then teased Joe by performing fellatio on the lucky snowman before she snapped shut her teeth and bit the end off the carrot. Joe winced and fell over in the snow holding his crotch as if it had been his own penis that had been decapitated.

As Jennie went to check if he was ok, Joe grabbed her and pulled her in. The two kissed eagerly as they rolled down the slope. Covered in compacted snow they needed no words. The gaze between them was enough to trigger a run back indoors and another go at screaming the house down.

"AI and algorithms are a bit like DNA in a murder case. People think they are so clever, they can't be wrong."
Det. Sgt. Simon Collins *(West Lancashire Police)*

The sun started to fill the bedroom with light at about 8:15 am. Such was the excitement of being together in this winter wonderland the last thing on their minds was to draw the curtains. Jennie stretched out her arms and tightened her muscles.

She could not think of a time in her life when she had felt happier. Not even during Christmases as a child. She had always got everything she'd ever asked for. Christmas for Jennie was always a happy affair. But this one, right here and right now, she felt complete. It was as if everything she had ever done in her life was about getting to this moment.

Joe was still fast asleep as Jennie slowly got out of the love palace. She went and had a pee before walking naked through to the kitchen and setting the coffee machine to create a pot of hot wake me up. She took a couple of packs of protein breakfast drinks out of the cupboard and set them on the side for when her prince awoke. Jennie returned to the bedroom to collect her dressing-gown.

Gathered in the folds of her fluffy comfort coat, hugging a black coffee, Jennie sat in the observation room and watched in complete contentment as the world began to shine. She didn't hear Joe get up, pour himself a coffee and prepare the breakfast drinks. It was a lovely surprise. The pair enjoyed a moment of pure relaxation together. No need for words or glances. Just the fact they had each other was enough.

Caught up in the moment the couple lost all track of time. It was only the arrival of the *MinzPyz™ Surpryz™* drone that pulled them back to this realm. It was Jennie who spotted it first, hovering just outside the window with its *Payload of Smiles™* suspended underneath. Jennie gave an excited squeal that alerted Joe to the flying object. He went and got the key to open the front door while Jennie ran into the living area.

Joe signed for the exquisitely wrapped gifts and removed them from the drone's payload. One was much heavier than the other. He tried to have a quick look at the name tags but was interrupted by Jennie yelling through from the other room.

"You better not be looking whose is whose."

He thought better of his action and proceeded to the living area where Jennie sat on one of the couches with her legs tucked under her. She wore the expression of an excited child: a look she pulled off very well indeed.

"The real question you should be asking when you enter into a relationship isn't how well do you know your partner, or how well does your partner know you? It's how well do you really know yourself?"
Dr Gail Nash *(T.V. Celebrity Relationship Expert)*

The coffee table became the designated prezzie zone. Joe placed the two festively-wrapped parcels on the table and gestured to Jennie to open first.

"No, you first." Jennie pushed the big heavy box toward Joe.

Joe picked up the package and judged the weight. *Quite a hefty and probably expensive thing,* he thought. Then he checked the name tag.

"It's not for me," he smiled as he handed it back to Jennie.

Curiously Jennie slowly tore at the paper. Joe did the same with the smaller box, only with less confusion. Once he had got past the paper wall of Santas in a regular pattern he found a box printed with multiple logos from his favourite films. Inside there were toy figures, miniature versions of his heroes. All of which he had not managed to add to his collection. At the bottom of the box he noticed a small golden figure in a plastic bag. At first, he thought he was seeing things but very quickly realised it was what he thought it was. He reached in and lifted it out. Through tear-filled eyes he found himself staring at a mint condition, though not in packaging, 1977 See-Threepio (C-3PO). It was the last one he needed to complete his collection of the original Kenner *Star*

Wars 12 backs. He looked over at Jennie and showed her the toy droid that he'd been looking for.

Jennie looked less pleased. Her expression was no longer that of a child mesmerised by the magic of Christmas. Staring into the box opened on her lap she looked like she was questioning the very point of existence. Her expression was a cross between disappointment, confusion and disbelief.

For a moment Joe didn't know what to do. He put down his droid and placed a hand on Jennie's leg. Jennie looked up from the box and stared at Joe as he tried to comfort her.

"Hey babe, you know sometimes they get it wrong..."

His platitudes were halted as she produced from the box a Fellmark Damascus Steel Bushcraft Axe. The steelhead glistened in the light. He could see from the way she held the beautifully crafted rosewood handle that it was perfectly weighted to her grip.

When they make mistakes, he thought, *they really do make mistakes.*

Jennie swung her legs out and stood up. The axe looked as light as a feather in her hand. Joe also stood up. The atmosphere in the room had changed dramatically and Joe was lost for what to do next.

"Like I said," he could hear the concern in his own voice, "it's just a mistake. We'll email them and they'll get it sorted out in the next hour or so."

"No!" There was a seriousness to Jennie's reply, "These boffins, the ones that write these apps and algorithms, they are very clever."

"Yeah babe, but..."

"No, but!" Jennie turned around to face her beau.

"They have all the data. They know everything about us. They know more about me than I know about myself. This isn't a mistake, it's a gift based on everything I have written and shared and liked and commented on."

"So, what does this mean then? You want to cut down trees?"

"I think..." She looked at the axe, then back at Joe. He could see tears forming in her eyes. "I know I love you, but I think this is what I truly want. Deep down. It's telling me I..." She paused to consider her next words, "That my real feelings are that I want to kill you."

Panic mixed with disbelief rushed through Joe's body. "Hang on! These things can't be 100% accu..."

Joe's words turned into a scream as Jennie smashed down the axe on the coffee table. It just brushed past Joe's arm. When it came to splintering the furniture the small plastic communications droid was no match for Damascus steel. The shiny gold miniature exploded under the force of the blow and shards scattered across the room.

There was no time to mourn. Joe leapt over the couch and headed straight for the bathroom next to the bedroom with the single beds. He slammed the door behind him, locked it and then pressed his weight against the handle's edge.

Joe's voice betrayed the utter panic and fear he was feeling, "Why are you doing this?"

"Because, deep down," she sounded calm, though obviously breathing quite deeply, "even though I love you, I must want you dead."

"No, wait!"

The sound of wood splintering and cracking accompanied the appearance of the axe head through the door, narrowly missing Joe's hand. He stepped back as more blows smashed their way through the door. With each blow of steel on wood, he could hear Jennie shouting.

"They. Are. Never. Wrong!"

Once a gap had been created in the splintered door, the love of his life pushed her face up to the opening. Her eyes were no longer the love-struck gaze of a star-crossed lover. Now she was wild and insane. There was fury and bloodlust in her smile.

"Here's Jennie!"

Joe reached out and picked up the first thing he could lay his hands on a can of hairspray. He pointed it at the crazy killer trying to break in and pressed. The fixing lacquer propelled from the compressed canister and coated Jennie's eyes.

The instant pain caused Jennie to throw back her head and reach for her face. She lost her grip on the axe which twisted as it fell and caught Jennie's thigh. The sharp Damascus steel edge sliced deep into her flesh. Blood started to flow.

Joe unlocked the door and pulled it open. He stopped for a moment. Jennie was holding her face and screaming in pain while lying in a pool of her own blood. Confusion rattled him. In that moment all he wanted to do was help. All he wanted to do was stop the bleeding, hold her and tell her everything was going to be alright. Joe inched forward and started to reach down to Jennie.

Quickly, she grabbed for the axe and swung it at Joe.

Her eyes were puffy and red. The manic smile had become the grimace of a monster. No more words. The axe was accompanied by guttural screams, something primaeval. Her injury was stopping her from standing and the flailing axe was making it difficult for Joe to escape.

He felt the same crushing sadness usually experienced by people who lose family members to dementia. Here was the face, the body, the sound and smell of someone he loved but she had the mind of someone unrecognisable.

He readied himself before whispering, "I love you."

He stepped forward trying to avoid the axe.

Jennie's actions were violent and unpredictable. Lashing out into spaces with no precision. Joe was not sure which way the axe was going with the next attempted strike and, as he tried to jump over her, Jennie caught him on the back of his calf. Pain shot up his body and caused him to fall forward. His momentum slid him further away from Jennie across the tiles.

Fear overrode the pain. As blood pumped from his wound Joe scrambled to his feet and found the keys to open the back door. Still dressed in his loungewear, with nothing on his feet, Joe stumbled as quickly as he could out onto the covered terrace. He turned to see Jennie climbing to her feet. Her blood-soaked dressing-gown had pulled open as it stuck to the sticky crimson puddle on the floor. Once she had steadied herself, Jennie took the axe in both hands and started to give chase.

Joe looked down at his own wound. A puddle of gore was forming around his foot and a small jet of blood pulsated with every beat of his heart. He started to move around the building towards the front of the house. But his wound, blood loss, and the sudden feeling of the cold reduced his capability. Just as he reached the side of the house, Jennie was on him again.

She swung the axe for his head. Taking evasive action

Joe ducked under the blow and, using the momentum of the swing, he pushed Jennie onto the ice rink. With no shoes on Jennie slipped over. She smacked her head, cracking her skull on the hard, frozen water. The impact split the skin on her temple causing blood to splatter at the point of impact before leaving a bright red streak across the white of the ice as she continued to slide. Eventually, she came to a halt, lying on her back, her dressing gown fully open exposing her naked blood-covered body to the cold air.

Tears started to fall on to Joe's cheeks as he stepped backwards away from the scene. Full of grief, and weakened by the loss of blood, Joe didn't look where he was stepping. Suddenly the world turned upside down as he fell backwards down the steps landing on his back. Completely disoriented, he started to drag himself down the path and onto the snow-covered garden. Exhausted, Joe stopped and rolled over onto his back. The white clouds hung still in the winter's air and he knew there was nothing else he could do.

The light of the sky suddenly darkened as the silhouette of Jennie, open dressing gown, axe above her head, filled his vision. Blood loss and cold took hold of the wild axe-wielding woman. She fell to her knees between Joe's legs. The axe slipped from her grip and fell behind her. With her last breath, she fell forward on to the prone Joe. Unable to move the last moment of Joe's life was spent staring into the face of Jennie, his one true love.

"The ability to choose who we worship, choose who we love, choose anything. That's what being sentient is about. The day we give ourselves over to all this AI and deep learning will be the day we finally give up on our free will."
Gordon Silvester *(Fryer at the Cottage Fish & Chip shop)*

"It's asking the question; how much do you trust apps?"
(reprise)

The final words fell from Samantha's lips like triumphant soldiers returning from war. She drew in a deep breath and smiled. There was nothing more she could do right now. All that was left was to sit back and wait for the verdict. There was a beat of silence before the sound of Ms Nikita applauding came through with her southern states tones.

"Oh, I do like that. Yes, I do."

Tears of pride and joy welled up in Samantha's eyes as she tried desperately to contain her excitement. Ms Nikita was very aware of what this had meant to Samantha.

"You just let them emotions go, honey," she placed her cigar in the skull ashtray, "and let me just say, from this Southern Belle to you, my English Rose, I'm excited to have you on board. If you agree to join me that is."

That was Samantha's cue to bounce up and down in her seat while making joyous squeaking noises. In a moment she would regain composure, but for now, for these few seconds, she was going to let years of rejection disappear in her scream of delight. This was two fingers up at all the teachers that said she would never amount to much. It was also a massive hug for Mrs Chatfield, the only teacher that ever encouraged her.

"I'm so pleased you liked it."

"Oh Sammy," Ms Nikita sat back in her chair, "I've been a fan ever since you wrote that blog about me. I have followed your work closely ever since. Now we need to get this here little ol' contract signed up."

"Sure." Samantha shook herself down to engage

business mode. "Is it a PDF with digital signature or do I have to wait for a hard copy?"

"Technology is a wonderful thing these days. I take it you received my package?"

"I did."

"Open it up there."

Samantha used the Cardiff Castle letter opener she bought on a school trip to cut the seal. After removing a couple of plastic bags and a ton of polystyrene, she pulled out a small electronic device with the words *Quill 1.4* written down the side in small red letters. Its footprint was about the size of a business card with a height of about ten millimetres. On the top was a pad that looked like the fingerprint scanner on her smartphone. Out of the back was a black USB lead.

"Now you just go ahead and plug it into your computer there."

Samantha did as instructed.

"Now open up your email and have a look at the PDF I've just sent over. You need to scroll all the way to the bottom of the document." Ms Nikita smiled, "If you're happy to sign, just place your thumb on the little ol' pad there."

This was all Samantha had ever wanted. She wasn't worried about getting ripped off, she just wanted to be recognised. She used the wheel on her mouse to scroll all the way down through pages and pages of legal spiel. Eventually, she reached the bottom where the words *Now place your thumb on the supplied signing pad* were written in a nice friendly typeface.

Samantha abided without hesitation. A short-lived pain shot through the end of her thumb. It was sharp and intense. As she recoiled she noticed a small needle retracting back into the device. Her thumbprint had a tiny droplet of blood in the centre. She instinctively raised the thumb to her mouth to suck away the bleed. A window popped up over the document declaring the contract to have been signed. Ms Nikita smiled, though now her demeanour was more firm and business-like.

"It's great to have you onboard Sammy. We'll be in touch again real soon."

A sense of melancholy fell over Samantha as the video feed cut leaving only the words, *Meeting has ended.*

"It's a story of regret."

The spoils of success glistened in the LA sun as Peter Cardoon opened the blind of his corner office with the remote control. He loved the way his awards sparkled in the morning. It was one of life's little pleasures that he always promised himself he would never get bored of. That and his view of the city. In a town full of stars he was famous; but to the wider world, he was invisible.

With people hanging on every word the sun-kissed mega stars said, it was more often than not Peter's words that were being heard. He was the go-to man when a script wasn't quite working, the fixer of speeches and the scribe of TV monologues that were shared far and wide across the internet.

All without his name on the credits.

The gold statues he had on his shelf came from industry awards. These prizes were accompanied with rather nice sized cheques and notoriety in the halls of power, but they weren't international fame. They were *recognition* and a *massive thank you* from those the writer had made look good or funny or clever. Although Peter was proud of every single award, and he was grateful for the lifestyle that came from being paid well for his skills, he craved public fame.

He wanted so much to be seen in the world, with his name as the writer, rather than the vain director who wanted both credits to make his talent look greater. Peter wanted to be studied at college in media lessons. He wanted his work to be held up as perfect examples of *pathos* and *ethos*. He wanted to be an inspiration to others. Even though his work was often cited as the reason others got into the industry and started to write, it was always with someone else's name on his words. It would be all *'Steven Steiner is a genius'* and *'I want to be just like him.'*

Peter growled into his cup of coffee, "When, actually, they want to be like me."

He placed his cup down on his desk next to the keyboard. The city stretched out in front of him and he smiled. Today was going to be the day all that changed. In a few minutes, he would be sitting down and having a meeting about his latest story idea. Only this time he would be the one getting the credit, he would be the one critics called, *'the new Shakespeare'*. This was his time to step out of the shadows and push his already successful career into the circle of fame he had always craved.

A gentle tap on his office door caught Peter's attention. *This was it, time to step forward*. He double-checked his clothing and brushed off any dust that might have fallen upon him. The mirror on the wall, so often used to straighten a bow tie, was perfect to ensure he had no breakfast remnants on his teeth.

The light tap on the door repeated.

Peter placed his hand on the handle and whispered to himself, "Welcome to the future." He opened the door and made immediate and purposeful eye contact. "Ms Nikita!" Shock flattened his smile, "What are you doing here?"

"Well a little ol' bird told me you had a new story," she stepped forward into the room, "and I've come to have a listen."

Quantumphrenia
By
Peter Cardoon

The streets of Manchester can feel cold, even at the height of the hottest of summers. The people wear the clothing appropriate to the weather, short-sleeves, shorts, loose-fitting dresses, wide-brimmed hats or baseball caps. The sun beats down on the commuters bustling their way to various destinations: work, home, drug dealer, university, or all of the above.

They have to wear the highest level of sunscreen to protect themselves from the harmful rays that have gotten stronger over the years. Rates of skin cancer keep rising year on year and even though everyone knows the dangers, people still try to brown their flesh because it makes them look good in photos on *Instafame*.

But the streets of Manchester can feel very cold. In all the activity, amongst all these people, in all this sunshine, the feeling amongst the population is not one of euphoria, it is one of loneliness and paranoia. The famous Northern *warmth* that had once welcomed so many, had been replaced with the stark, self-contained suspicion that had seen people become less social in public as they became more social online.

This was a society cultivated by the government. The new regime had rewarded those that gave information about their neighbours. It actively encouraged people to interact more online than in person. This way the government could monitor what people were talking about and learn who was plotting what. Consequently, talking in public was seen as sinister. If you didn't want to participate online you obviously had something to hide. So, people stopped talking on the streets, in shops and pubs. After-work groups disbanded as everything disappeared behind phone screens.

These strangers in a crowd might even be friends or follow each other's digital life, but outside of the superhighway, they were anonymous to each other. Society had become blind to itself, which suited Dr Matthew Wells. He liked being able to go about his business without anyone noticing. No one was interested in who he was, or what did. His work could carry on in secret with no interference. No authorities threatening to close him down: despite it being against the law.

It was the extra powers afforded to the Prime Minister to help tackle the climate crisis, without having to always consult parliament, that brought about the rise to power of Jason Abbot: the UK's last Prime Minister and first President. He used these powers to strip away the democratic process, eventually shutting down parliament and declaring it 'Not fit for purpose.'

Once installed as the President, he then dismantled the power of the Royal family and the House of Lords. This was far easier to do than anyone had imagined. A few pokes in the right-populist ribs, via the right-populist media outlets, and four referendums later, just to confirm, President Abbot became the sole lawmaker of the United Kingdom.

At first, people rebelled, looking up from their screens for a moment to voice their dissatisfaction. There were marches and sit-ins. Weeks of protests, all screaming in horror at the death of democracy. But soon, once the full force of this cruel and unrelenting governance was stamped down hard, people soon fell in line.

Now the streets of Manchester felt cold, along with every other city, town and village in the country. People were too scared to converse outside the internet, lest they be taken to the camps for 're-patriot training'. It is a way of life that has been the norm for the last decade. Each new law being designed to control every aspect of society, delivering a *mostly* compliant population.

By publishing bogus research papers that neither give any new insight nor disprove anything in the common mind, Dr Wells's existence was largely a footnote. He had an online profile and was a member of a number of very conventional groups. He expressed opinions that were designed to be ignored. There was nothing remarkable about his online life. Nothing to make him stand out in either a positive or negative way. Matthew was very much a no one, as he had planned to be. This was a wall he had built so that he could carry on his research.

Before *Abbot's Dawn,* Dr Wells was a leading researcher and theorist in the field of Fourth Dimensional Navigation. His ideas were the subject of many debates. That was until the Abbot government outlawed all research into time travel. It was one of those strange announcements that, to the main population, seemed like a completely pointless thing to do. For the scientists working in this field, a field from which funding had just been removed, it was devastating. But Dr Wells was too far into his research to stop, so he carried on, in secret. He covered his tracks and hid in plain sight. He just never shared his ideas with anyone except his lab assistant, Carrie.

In the real world, where online was the only place a person could legally meet to discuss anything from football to political views, all gender identity rights had been banned. President Abbot laid out his beliefs at a community centre hustings on his campaign trail.

"I personally believe that what you are born is what you are. Be that homosexual, bisexual or heterosexual, it matters not. But what does matter, what is important is that a man is a man and a woman is a woman. For too long we have given ourselves over to confusion, and the PC fascists, telling us that we should let our children be who they want. To identify as whatever they want. Well, my son wants to be Doctor Who and he can neither be as much that, as a man can be a proper woman."

This speech became known as the Rottingdean Address. Many denounced it as right-wing hyperbole. Then he won the election and people were stunned. It took a couple of years for the Abbot administration to start bringing in legislation. Staying true to his word, much to the delight of his supporters, the then Prime Minister Abbot introduced a law banning 'The practice and encouragement of Transgenderism.' The world was shocked. The law polarized the divide in society and was the third such directive to encourage people to spy on their neighbours.

While the debate raged in those academic circles in which Dr Wells moved, he was not surprised by anything Jason Abbot did. With each new restriction, power grab, and removal of freedom, Matthew would just tell his colleagues. "He was a little shit when I knew him at junior school, he's no different now."

So, when he started to work in secret and needed an assistant, he told Trevor Lord, one of his undergraduates, he could work the lab as himself. No need to hide. Trevor was shocked that Dr Wells knew he was trans in the first place, but then accepted the post as Carrie.

Dr Wells and Carrie had been working on a form of time travel using Quantum Entanglement. The machine Dr Wells had designed, and which he had built with the help of Carrie, wasn't something that could move physical forms, it wasn't a matter transfer device. The machine couldn't send any modern technology back in time. No clothes or watches. No computers or phones. No guns or weapons of any kind. The machine that Dr Wells had created could transfer the state of one particle, or several million particles to be precise, from one World Point to another in a Closed Timelike Curve. Or, in other words, Dr Wells had developed the ability to transfer the present-day consciousness of an individual back in time to switch places with their younger self.

All the memories of now remained intact, meaning the traveller would essentially know the future. On their return, the traveller would remember in the present but have a blank moment in the past. The only recall of events of the time spent in the past would be from the present consciousness. That had been the theory, and after successful testing, Dr Wells and Carrie could confirm that was also a fact. Several times, Dr Wells had returned to a point in his past, making sure he didn't hit any major events in his life.

The first time he travelled back he wasn't sure what was going to happen. He decided to work with extremes and travel back as far as he could. This resulted in him becoming aware of being in his mother's womb. He was overwhelmed by the warm, safe feeling. He could hear his mother's heartbeat and feel the rush as her blood flowed through his body. The trip lasted less than a minute. It took Matthew five days to recover from the experience. This trip had taught him one major thing. You cannot travel back further than your own conception.

A couple more experiments followed. On his second trip, he was more aware of the journey. The first time it felt like he closed his eyes in the present and woke up in the past. However, this wasn't the case. The second time he noticed that he had a split second where he could see the journey. It was like a tunnel made up of various shades of white light. Through this angelic corridor of energy, Dr Wells could see a blue streak which continued after he dropped out into his teenage years.

After a couple more trips he could determine that these blue streaks were like breadcrumbs of his mind, paths he had taken through time.

Carrie had a go. She returned to her 14th birthday party when, as a young boy, she felt disconnected from everyone. This time she was able to have more fun, but not enough to upset the timeline. After Carrie's trip, Dr Wells noticed an orange streak. *This must be Carrie's line,* he thought. This led to the second revelation: you can tell where travellers have been.

Dr Wells most recent experiment led to the third revelation about time travel. On this occasion, he wanted to know if it was possible to travel into the future. To get a glimpse of what was to come.

Sitting in the general examination chair Dr Wells had 'borrowed' from the university's medical department stores, and modified for his own experimental needs, Matthew gave Carrie the nod to proceed. She strapped his arms and legs into position. This was done as a precaution. During one of Dr Wells's first attempts, he had experienced muscle spasms. His flailing arms smashing him in the nose, breaking it. This had caused him to fall out of the chair and do further damage to his head and body whilst convulsing on the floor. Even though this reaction had never happened again, once Matthew returned to the lab after eight weeks of bed rest, he insisted on being strapped in.

Carrie ran through the procedural list. She gave the computer log the title 'Future Trip Experiment 1.' She switched the power on and took notes as she observed the Doctor's reactions.

Dr Wells' vision instantly changed from the bright examination lights of the secret lab in the Basement of Manchester University's Nuclear Research Department to the bright buzzing active surroundings of the 'Time Tunnel'. His control over his movements here had been getting better. Observing the various paths back he turned to try and travel the other way. All he could see was a wall of energy, like looking at the surface of the Sun. He made an attempt to move through the wall but as he touched it the energy soared through his very being. Every atom in his body, in his mind, lit up like the stars in the night's sky. Instantly he was back in the lab, screaming in pain. His heart was pumping so hard it took a moment before he could hear Carrie shouting at him.

"Are you OK? Wells? Can you hear me? Matthew?"

Once he had recovered he was able to tell Carrie what he had seen and felt, going into as much detail as he could so she could write it up in the log. Carrie then told the Doctor what she had seen.

At first, all seemed normal. The readings were as expected and Dr Wells' vital signs were just what she wanted to see. Then something she had never witnessed before occurred. The Doctor's vital signs dropped to nothing. When she looked over at him in the chair she could see him, but she could also see the equipment behind him. He was translucent: like a ghost.

The doctor pulsed, fading in and out of opacity until suddenly he screamed and was solid again. The last line of the log for 'Future Trip Experiment 1', was, 'The third revelation of time travel is; you cannot travel further into the future than your own set present.'

That was three weeks ago. The future experiment had caused minor damage to the equipment so Dr Wells and Carrie had been spending most of their time repairing and recalibrating the sensors. Everything was set for them to resume their experiments. Even though they had successfully travelled back in time on several occasions, more data was needed.

Dr Wells gave his lectures on 'Particle Physics and Quantum Field Theory', something he had to do four times a year as part of his contract with the university. Once he had finished and spent some time chatting with colleagues to keep his face known amongst the faculty, he returned to his lab.

As he got to the door of the basement he was greeted by Carrie, though she was still dressed as Trevor and had genuine fear in her voice.

"You are not going to believe this Doctor."

They entered the lab. Sat in the examination chair was a ghost figure, pulsating, fading though not coming back to full opacity. Each pulse returned to a weaker image. By the time Dr Wells had moved across the room, it had faded completely. Carrie broke the silence.

"That was…"

"President Jason Abbot, yes." Dr Wells examined the chair. "There is no residue. Check the log."

Carrie logged onto the computer system. There was nothing there, nothing at all. Their entire hard drive had been wiped. Everything was gone. All the videos, audio files. Every document, log and reading: there was nothing.

"No need for tears Carrie, everything is backed-up."

"How do you know they didn't get to those files as well?"

"I'm not talking about the back-ups you know about. I have some very secure data banks on the cloud hidden behind a very tough VPN."

"How come? Don't you trust me?"

"It wasn't you. I didn't trust the university and by the look of this, I had good reason." He moved across to the computer, "Now let's download the code again and reboot."

To the pair of scientists, the reinstalling and rebooting sequence seemed to take an age. Eventually, the Quantum Regulator fired up and the countdown could begin. Dr Wells sat in the chair.

"Strap me in and run the sequence."

"What are you going to do?"

"If my suspicions are correct this was his first trip." Matthew started to put the monitors on himself, "Which means he won't know about the paths. I know he might have read our logs but I know Abbot from our school days and reading wasn't his first love. He was very clever but very lazy. If he's gone back far enough, I can follow."

Carrie tightened the Doctor's straps and attached the last of the electrodes. She triple-checked the code sequencing. She then ran five quantum entanglement models to ensure the numbers were running correctly. Each part of the sequence was checked and checked again. However keen they were to find out what was going on, they knew that one slip up here could be catastrophic. The countdown was at 5.

"4… 3… 2… 1…"

Carrie pressed the two final buttons at exactly the same time.

In this second she realised that the president couldn't have done this alone. As Dr Wells entered the Time Tunnel, Carrie became aware of the two very large, very imposing men that had just walked through the door.

"Good luck Doctor," she whispered. "It was an honour."

Deep in the quantum cylinder of the time tunnel, Dr Wells didn't hear the shot. He didn't see Carrie's brains splatter against the equipment. He was unaware of the damage they were doing to his life's work to stop him from being able to return, and he was unaware that they had been acting on the president's orders. Even though the president wasn't sure why he had given those orders.

In the time tunnel, Dr Wells could see the green path left by Abbot, though it was fading, like it was being erased. Focusing on the line, Dr Wells followed it and, using the skills he had mastered over the years, he managed to dip back into the timeline very close to the time where Abbot had returned.

*****

Morning was breaking through the crack in the curtains. Matthew opened his eyes and gazed up at the ceiling that he had not seen for many years. On all his previous visits Dr Wells had managed to avoid returning home. He heard movement coming from the bed on the other side of the room. Looking over he saw his older brother getting out of bed. By the look of him, naked bar for a pair of purple Y-fronts with white trims, his brother was about 15 years old. That meant Matthew was 12. So, Abbot was definitely heading back to his early school days. But why?

Matthew got out of bed and looked down at what he was wearing. He hadn't worn pyjamas since he was 14 and, even though the idea of sleeping naked hadn't entered his thoughts at this point in his timeline, his much older consciousness made him aware of how uncomfortable he felt. Then came the reason why he had avoided returning home in all his previous visits. His mum's voice.

"Come on, get out of bed, breakfast in ten minutes."

Without any decipherable words, the unmistakable sound of his dad's voice mumbled in the background saying something that made his mother laugh.

In the time he had just come from they were both dead. His father died many years before his mum. Taken by illness before he was able to enjoy retirement with grandkids. His mother, on the other hand, lived to a good age. Though she often wished she hadn't hit the brakes so hard the day a ten-year-old Jason Abbot ran out in front of her car.

"If I knew then what I know now, things would be very different."

It was her claim to fame in the old people's home and she would tell the story to anyone who would listen. It kept her amused and young enough in mind to last to nearly 100. She was so close to getting a telegram from President Abbot. Matthew was convinced that she died 3 days before her century just to "Spite the little shitbag," as she had promised to do on many occasions.

Still trying to get his bearings, Dr Wells (although it would be many years before he would get his PhD) picked up the clothes left out for him by his mum. A simple pale blue t-shirt, a pair of black trousers, grey socks and white Y-fronts.

Matthew remembered this kind of attire: *this must be a school day*, he thought.

Matthew had just finished getting dressed when his brother came back into the room with his hand down the front of his underpants scratching his genitals. He removed his hand and wiped it on Matthew's hair.

"Morning spaz."

When Matthew had the mind of a twelve-year-old this would have upset him. He would have probably run into the kitchen to complain in a very whiny manner about what had just happened. Exaggerating the level of disgust and insisting that Paul was picking on him. But with an older mind, he just found it funny. Like a warm memory which he was living again.

Matthew left the bedroom and walked down the hallway to the kitchen on the left. The muffled sounds of shouting filtered through from the flat upstairs. It was a normal occurrence of his childhood, although they did seem to have started early today.

He ate his breakfast in silence. The sight of his parents had been more emotional than he had anticipated. By not speaking much he was able to keep the tears in check. Matthew also had the thoughts of finding Jason to help focus his mind.

Once the morning eating was done, Matthew picked up his school bag and left the flat for the short walk to school. The sun was bright and the hills of the South Downs that surrounded Hollingbury were green and lush. The smell of the Sussex air evoked memories of summers past, though from this point in time some of those were memories of summers yet to come. Paul dished out one last insult before heading off in the direction of Patcham Fawcett High School up on the hill across from the factory units. Matthew headed down Chelwood Close towards Carden Juniors.

It was in these grey walls that Matthew had come back and visited the most. Though on this trip he had already spent more time in the past than ever before. The previous visits to this time involved him suddenly becoming aware that he was sat in a lesson. Without drawing any attention to himself he just looked around, observed his surroundings then returned to the lab. His longest mission until this one had been sixty-five seconds. This time, he was walking around in his past. Pretty soon he was going to have to talk to others. Children that, from their perspective, would have only spoken to him yesterday. Yet it had been many years since his last interaction with any of them. He didn't even attend the school reunion.

The playground was busy, as he remembered. A group of girls were playing skipping games over in the corner near the school building. A gang of boys played football in the middle of the tarmac. Tracy Beakon ran across the field of play, tackled Johnathon Wheel, dispossessing him before skilfully dribbling the ball around four other boys and scoring past the hapless Sean Spencer in goal. This started a row about how girls shouldn't be playing football. Another very normal occurrence as Matthew recalled.

He smiled and turned to view the rest of the children playing various games.

That was when he saw Jason. Sat on the wall over by the metal steps that lead to the top corridor. He was being very quiet, keeping himself to himself. Matthew walked over. As he got closer Jason looked up. Matthew could see immediately that those were not a child's eyes. Behind the brown irises, there was knowledge and experience. They were the eyes that no longer viewed the world with wonder.

Jason beckoned Matthew over to sit next to him. At first, this surprised Matthew but then he thought, *if I can see the older mind through his eyes, then vice versa?* As he approached, Jason stood up and offered his hand. Matthew took it and the pair shook like a couple of old business acquaintances. Jason spoke first. His words had the structure of an adult, but the pitch of a child whose voice was yet to break.

"So, you did follow me. I wasn't quite sure if you would."

"When the President of the United Kingdom disappears before your eyes, on a time machine that said President has declared as being illegal, one must investigate."

"Oh, so I'm President, good. My plan seems to have worked better than I thought."

"Plan?"

Jason smiled, "You know for being such a celebrated boffin you can be quite thick."

"All I know is that I've been working in secret because you, as President of the UK, banned all research into time travel."

"And yet you carried on."

Matthew stopped to think about that. He had carried on, despite the ban. Had Abbot known about his work all along?

"You knew?"

"The future I came here from, I wasn't President, and you were the famous Dr Matthew Wells; inventor of time travel." Jason ran his fingers through his hair. "I was sitting in a prison cell reading your published research when it hit me. If I could go back with the knowledge I had in my head, I could excel at school. Give myself an advantage."

"But you would change the timeline and as such lose the knowledge."

"Ah yes, I read your paper. But that will only happen after I have managed to get higher grades and move up to high school in a much better class. By the time I forget all of this, which I will as the future changes, I will have already set my new course. When I leave Carden in eight weeks, I will have boosted my chances of future success." He stared at Matthew straight in the eye, "And by the sounds of it, my plan worked."

"What if I just don't invent time travel? What if I stay here and find something else to be fascinated about?"

"We both know that will never happen."

A tone of defeat entered Matthew's voice, "Because we are having this conversation. The fact this is happening now proves I will go on and invent time travel."

"You know, I never used to believe in fate."

Jason stood up and walked off without saying another word. Matthew stared at his shoes. His mind was racing with idea after idea trying to think of a way of stopping him. He now knew that the future he had come from had been altered. That before Abbot went back to this point the world was different. He didn't know if it was better than the one he left, but he was damned sure it couldn't be any worse. Matthew took in a deep breath and gazed across the playground to help with the thinking process. Sat on the bench opposite him he saw Wendy Parkinson. That's when it struck him. He now knew what he had to do.

Matthew spent the rest of the day going through the motions of the school day. He sat in class half listening to what was being said by the teacher just in case he was asked any questions. Though he needn't have worried. At every given opportunity Jason Abbot was the first to impress. Each time he used his advanced knowledge he would be praised. And each time he was praised he looked over at Matthew and smiled.

The day passed without incident. Matthew had managed to avoid any real contact with anyone. He supplied simple one-word answers when conversing with his old friends, not engaging with any classroom activities. He stayed under the radar and out of Abbot's way. When the bell rang for the end of the day, Matthew headed straight home. His old friends gathered at the local shop as he passed unnoticed.

Being a latchkey kid, and having a brother that spent most of his time playing football, meant Matthew would be returning to an empty flat, which was perfect. He needed time to work out his plan. He knew that if everything stayed the same, he would still go on to invent this process and Abbot's plan would again be fulfilled.

His next thought was to return to the lab. From there he could calculate the time needed to go backwards and then stop Abbot getting to the machine. However, every time he tried to return there was nothing. He soon realised that his lab in the future had been destroyed. Abbot had trapped him here to ensure his plan would be successful. Then Matthew realised that this also probably meant that Carrie had been hurt, or even worse, killed. This only steadied Matthew's resolve to end this by any means necessary.

"What if I'm not around?" he hypothesized. "What if I put myself in a position where I can't develop this machine?"

Matthew looked out of his flat's ground floor bedroom window. It gave him a view down Chelwood Close towards the houses on the hill. Walking down the path towards the opposite block was Neil Wren. An old man in his 60s who would tell anybody about his days fighting in World War II while making them feel very uncomfortable.

Mr Wren had something Matthew needed. The young Dr Wells had remembered a time when a group of the children on the estate, led by the older boys, took great delight in annoying Wreny by throwing stones at his windows and shouting out abusive names they themselves didn't understand. It was all fun and games until he came to the window brandishing his old Enfield service revolver, threatening to shoot them all. They scattered, running in every direction possible.

No shots were fired but they never tried to taunt him again. It was that service revolver that Matthew now wanted to get his hands on, and he was willing to do whatever it would take to get it.

Even though the adults never explained why the children of the estate were told to stay away from Mr Wren's front door, even on 'Bob a job' week, it was well known amongst all the kids that Mr Wren enjoyed the company of youngsters, both boys and girls. Or, as Matthew's brothers put it one day when warning his little brother about that flat, "He. Is. A. Nonce! Stay away!"

Matthew changed his clothes from the trousers and t-shirts of school to something more akin to playing on the streets and fields of the area. He put on a pair of dark blue tracksuit bottoms which sported double white lines down the outside of each leg, and a t-shirt showing a highly detailed cartoon of pirates on a pirate ship.

The world seemed distant, almost dreamlike as Matthew left his flat and took the short walk to the other block. Standing at only three floors it wasn't the size of the buildings that made them imposing: it was the way all the blocks were at differing heights as they were constructed on plateaus carved into the steep hillside. Matthew walked down the concrete steps that lead to the entrance hall.

Inside the block was identical to the one where he lived. Grey shiny polished concrete floors gave access to the two flats opposite each other on this floor. There was a door to the rear of the building, which the kids used to run through when playing some sort of chase game, or escaping annoyed adults. The walls had recently been painted beige with a multicoloured spittle effect in an attempt to brighten them up, but the paint job could not get rid of that damp stone smell that hung as an undertone to the air.

The stairs leading to the second floor were made out of the same polished concrete as the floor with hard, sharp angles. The stairs went up towards the back of the building. As Matthew reached the top he had to turn to face the front again putting the flat he was interested in, Mr Wren's flat, on the right. He approached the door. There was a feeling of nervous nausea of a level Matthew could not recall ever having experienced before. He had felt nervous when he first presented his theory on time travel to his university professor as an excited twenty-one-year-old. He felt even more nervous on the day he got married. But neither of those came close to this.

His hand trembled as he knocked on the door. The sound of the brass fitting hitting the small metal plate echoed through the block before the air returned to creepy uncomfortable silence. Through the wooden door, Matthew could hear Mr Wren moving. It seemed to take him an age to reach the door. Rattling sounds of the chain being applied and the lock being turned seemed amplified. The door opened as far as the safety chain would allow and Mr Wren's face appeared in the gap.

His deep soft voice sounded vulnerable. "What do you want?"

Matthew just smiled. A moment that lasted longer in Matthew's head than it did in reality, was broken when Mr Wren closed the door and removed the chain restriction. Slowly the old man opened the door and invited the child in. With his mind firmly on the bigger picture, Matthew entered the flat.

The layout was very much like his. Bathroom immediately to the left with the living room to the right. A hallway ran straight from the front door to a bedroom door facing. Up the hallway, the first door on the left was the kitchen with the second door on the wall led to another bedroom. Matthew shuffled over towards the bathroom to allow Mr Wren to close the door. As he looked across to the living room, he recognised the gun box displayed on top of a glossy rosewood sideboard. His granddad had one just the same, only he lived in Manchester.

Mr Wren smiled at Matthew. "Would you like a drink? Some juice?"

Matthew shook his head.

"Please come through." Mr Wren turned and walked through to the living room, "I don't get many visitors."

Trying not to look at the gun box Matthew walked through. The room again was like his own, only with different furniture. Mr Wren had no television, just a large radio on a small table next to the tatty looking chair at the opposite end of the room from the sideboard. The windows faced out towards the back like his own flat with an open coal fire on the other wall facing. There was a coffee table with various magazines piled neatly. Mr Wren pulled the curtains to remove the sunlight from the room before sitting down in the chair.

"Switch the light on, will you child?"

Matthew did as instructed.

"Now what brings you here?"

Matthew tried to think about how a child would speak, "I was told you might give me a pound."

"Sometimes, maybe."

"I wanted some sweets but my mum..."

"You must be very warm. Take off that t-shirt and cool yourself down."

The realisation of what was about to happen started to hit home. But Matthew couldn't think of any other way. He had to change the future, and this was a means to an end. Even though Matthew stripped down to his underpants, Mr Wren never touched him, only himself. The whole experience lasted no longer than ten minutes.

"You get dressed while I get you your pound."

This was his chance. Matthew pulled on his clothes as fast as he could and rushed over to the gun box. His heart sank when he saw the lock. He tried the lid anyway and found it was open. Inside was the dark grey weapon with six rounds. Frantically he pushed the ammunition into his pocket. One of the brass cases had other ideas and tried to jump back towards the box. Through the tangle of blue cloth and fingers, it fell to the floor. Suddenly Matthew's attention was drawn to the hallway, Mr Wren was coming back. Quickly Matthew shut the lid of the gun box and placed his foot over the lead tipped cartridge.

Mr Wren sheepishly entered the room. He looked at the boy who was red in the face and had the eyes of someone who was in fear of his life. The old man couldn't look at him. Full of shame he placed a one-pound note on the sideboard and trudged off back towards the bedroom without saying a word.

His heart beating faster and harder than during any cross-country run at school, Matthew stooped to pick up the rogue shell. Stopping to listen for Mr Wren, once he determined the old man wasn't returning, Matthew opened the box and picked up the gun. It was much heavier than he had anticipated. In his future, the doctor had handled a number of guns on a shooting range as part of his stag-do. Along with some old rifles they also had a go at a similar-looking revolver however, at the age of 12 his muscles were nowhere near the same strength and he almost dropped the weapon on the sideboard.

Getting a better grip on the gun Matthew shoved his hand up the front of his t-shirt to try and conceal it as best he could. He then remembered the pound note: leaving that would raise suspicion. He shoved it into his other pocket. The security chain hadn't been reset on the door which made it easy for a quick and quiet exit. Without stopping Matthew swiftly moved through the block, down the stairs and out of the building. The quickest place to go would have been home but, for what Matthew had in mind, home was not the place to be.

Next to the flats, lush green fields hugged the contours of the South Downs. Starting at the bottom of a hill a play park was built into the slopes. There were swings, roundabouts and a climbing frame, all designed to entertain the children of the estate, and all of which had been damaged by said children in some way. The shiny metal slide with wood cabin style logs had been reduced to just a frame, and the sandpit was more like the world's biggest cat litter tray. It still entertained the children though, just not in the way it was intended.

Above this was a well-kept field with daisies galore. One day it was a football pitch, the next a cricket ground. Badminton, tennis, hill rolling and spinning with your arms stretched out. This was a place of sports. Further up the hill and the environment changed. A wild area with overgrown grass and wild blackberries. Trees perfect for climbing with the added danger of a patch of stinging-nettles growing just underneath for extra damage to anyone who fell. The adventurous types would hunt in the long grass for slow worms, lizards and grasshoppers.

At the top of this unofficial nature reserve a fence divided the estate from the farmer's field, and in the top left corner of the long grass a crop of trees and bushes formed a natural den. This was a place away from everything. One side was almost fully covered in, bar for a small entrance in the branches. The other side was open to the landscape.

From here the view extended from the Stammer Forest all the way over to Patcham Fawcett High School. It was an escape that only a few kids knew about, and by the amount of discarded soft porn magazines often found here, it was also frequented by teenagers and the occasional adult.

It was to this camp that Matthew headed. Up over the field and through the long grass. Moving as quickly as he could without drawing any attention to himself. Only when he reached the camp did he stop. It was here, with the South Downs to bear witness, that Matthew fell to his knees and started to cry. This was the first moment where he was able to think about what just happened. Even though he knew what was going to happen, and his mind was much more capable of dealing with the situation. Even though he wasn't touched and it wasn't as bad as he had imagined, he still felt violated.

Once he had gathered his thoughts he pulled out the gun. The Enfield service revolver. It was dark grey with a redwood grip screwed to each side of the handle. Matthew found the lock and used the brake-action to open the gun, revealing the empty chambers of the revolving cylinder. He snapped it shut without putting any of the .38 cartridges in. Choosing various targets Matthew got used to the weight by pointing, aiming with the large forward sight on the muzzle and pulling the double-action trigger until the hammer snapped back with a click. He tried to cock it, like in the detective programmes he had seen on the TV, however, there was no spur on the hammer which made this impossible.

The firing action was much lighter than Matthew thought, as the gun itself felt heavy. After a few practice shots, Matthew broke the gun open again. This time, with a shaking hand, he loaded the bullets. Clicking it shut he weighed the weapon again in his hand. Somehow the pistol felt different, not just in the weight, but in the feel. This was no longer a clicking toy for killing pretend German soldiers or Martians. A pull on this trigger would end a life. The enormity of such power was tangible. Now he had to test a theory. He had to stop himself being in a position to invent time travel and he only had two ideas. This was the first one: to shoot himself.

However, Matthew was well aware that this might not be possible. Theoretically, the gun would malfunction as the universe protected itself from collapse. He had been there when the first experiments were done. A single-photon was sent back in time with the ability to destroy itself once it reached its destination. However, no matter how many times they ran the experiment, it always failed, even though when the now named 'Quantum Gun' was tested in the present it worked fine. This was all well and good, but he was a lot more than a single photon.

First he tried placing the muzzle against his temple. But he couldn't pull the trigger. It was like his hand just wouldn't do what it was told. Next he pushed the muzzle up under his chin, pressing it into the soft flesh so that it hurt. The muscles in his right arm tensed with the pressure but his fingers felt like stone. He screamed and held the gun against his chest with the muzzle pointing at his heart. This time it would be his thumb doing the deed, but still, he just couldn't move it that final millimetre.

He thought he'd have one more go, in the mouth this time, but before he scraped his teeth with the metal, he heard someone crying. Matthew hid the gun under some leaves and looked out. Wendy Parkinson was slowly walking toward the new red brick flats where she lived at the top of the estate. Those were not tears of pain. The way she was walking, her reluctant speed and the sheer sadness on her face told Matthew she didn't want to go home, and he knew why.

Her mother lived with a man called Gary. He was a nasty piece of work. Long after Matthew had left the estate he found out that Gary used to beat Wendy and her sister. Worst of all, the bastard raped her on her 15th birthday and continued to abuse her until she took her own life after his last assault on her 17th. This is what went through Matthew's mind when he saw her in the playground. This presented him with his second option: kill Gary and get arrested.

If Jason was trying to get a leg up with his knowledge,

placing him on a better educational path, Matthew was going to do the opposite. He would get himself put away in juvenile detention, not achieve his PhD and never have the opportunity to realise his greatest work. As an added bonus, he would save Wendy from years of hell and maybe save her life.

Retrieving the pistol from its cover Matthew left the camp and followed Wendy back home. Even these newer buildings followed the same layout as the post-war fabrication that decorated the hillside. The major visual difference was the use of red brick on the outside instead of the overlapping grey slabs. The communal entrance halls had the same dampness hanging in the air with the general unpleasant aroma. Sound bounced off the stark concrete floors and walls with the slight echo giving any voice an almost metallic character.

Two flights of solid stairs led up to Wendy's flat on the top floor. She had got back well ahead of Matthew. The front door was shut and locked.

Remembering an old trick that people used to do before everybody had more stuff to steal Matthew checked the letterbox in the middle of the door and investigated inside with his fingers. Just to the left he found what he was looking for: a length of string tied to a hook. Matthew pulled the string through the opening to find the front door key tied to the other end. Slowly he used it to gain entry to the flat.

This flat was on the opposite side of the landing to his and Mr Wren's. As he crept through, the bathroom was on his right with the living room to the left where the sounds of some TV programme were blaring out through the open door. Quietly Matthew tried to determine if there was anyone else in the place. There was definitely the sound of someone in the bedroom facing him at the end of the hall. The other bedroom door to the right was open. Matthew tried to see any signs of movement. There was nothing, not even a shadow. He watched the doorway to the kitchen with the same interest, again nothing. The bathroom door was wide open, so Matthew knew there was no one in there.

Crouching down, the young doctor sneaked up to the edge of the door of the living room and peered round to get the lay of the land. Sat with his back to the door in a comfy chair that had seen better days was Wendy's tormentor. In his left hand was a lit cigarette with a length of ash that looked like it needed tapping off into an ashtray. In his other hand was a blue can of Tennent's lager sporting the image of a woman in a red dress. The colour TV he faced was turned up loud enough to distort the sound of *the Human League* performing on some children's TV show. Suddenly Gary moved. The ash from his cigarette gave way and fell to the floor. The beer in his other hand also dropped to the carpet. The snoring sound coming from this vile man gave Matthew the signal that he was asleep.

Pointing the gun at Gary, Matthew walked around the chair and stood between the sleeping drunk and the *80s synth-pop band.*

Gary was slumped. A line of drool dripped from his mouth and by the look of the dark patch on his sweatpants, he had pissed himself. Tightening his grip on the Enfield, Matthew aimed at Gary's chest and slowly pulled the trigger.

Without the ear defenders of the range to muffle the sound, the controlled explosion used to propel the elongated 200-grain lead bullet down the muzzle was much louder than Matthew had anticipated. The recoil caused Matthew's arm to twitch upwards but not as much as he had expected. The result was that Matthew, even at this close range, had missed Gary's chest. The slight twitch, the act of closing his eyes when he fired, and the lack of experience in handling firearms meant that the shot hit Gary in the head.

There wasn't much change in Gary's sitting position, his shoulders had slumped a bit more. His head had fallen forward and blood was pouring out of the wound where his nose used to be. The bullet had created an exit wound larger than the entrance though it hadn't made it through the chair. Skull fragments and chunks of brain matter spread on the back of the chair like a Rorschach inkblot.

With the ringing in his ears from the bang, the smell of gunpowder from the discharged firearm and the composition of gore in front of him, Matthew fell to his knees and vomited what little he had in his stomach. He took deep breaths to try and gain some composure. The act of killing, however right the intention, had a massive impact. The surrealism of the room started to fade and clear thoughts were starting to return. Matthew looked over at the body. Standing just inside the room Wendy was surveying the scene.

Matthew remembered going to Wendy's 21st birthday party. He remembered getting an invite to her wedding. He also knew that he had travelled back in time to stop Jason, which meant Wendy never told anyone what he had done. She looked at Matthew kneeling on the floor.

"He sells drugs," there wasn't even a hint of fear in her voice, "They will think it was just some deal gone wrong kind of revenge killing."

She walked over to Matthew and offered a hand to helped him to his feet.

"You need to go now."

"What about you?"

"I'll just say I came home and found him." She kissed him on the cheek. "Thank you. Now go."

Matthew picked up the pistol and started towards the door. He turned for a moment to have one last look at Wendy to make sure she was OK. She was calm and had the look of both hate and satisfaction in her eyes as she stared at Gary's corpse. But the outcome was not what Matthew wanted. He had to think of another plan.

Swiftly and as quietly as he could, Matthew left Wendy's block. He ran towards the fields and headed for the border between the mowed hill and the long grass. Time was moving on and it wouldn't be long now before his parents were home. Matthew's brother Paul was with some of the other boys on the estate kicking a football about on the field at the bottom of the hill. He turned to look over at the block he lived in. Curiously, he saw Jason Abbot leaving the building. *But Jason lives up the top end of Carden Hill?* he thought.

As best he could, Matthew tried to conceal the gun in his tracksuit bottoms, something they were never designed to do. It was pointless so, despite the warm air, he returned home to get a coat. His parents weren't back yet. The atmosphere in the flat felt different to him now. He had killed a man, nothing was going to be the same again in his head and he still knew that Abbot was going to turn the world against itself in a paranoid dystopia.

The bathroom mirror gazed back at him as he tried to talk himself out of the only idea he could think of. The gun fitted snugly in his blue coat pocket. Leaving a note on the table saying *I'm having tea at Dylan's,* Matthew left to find Jason.

*****

As Jason left Matthew's block he headed towards the school, which could also have been his way home. *But why was he here?* Matthew decided to head in the same direction. He walked swiftly to the end of Chelwood Close and looked right, down the hill. There, on the other side of the upper school field, Jason was just starting to descend the stone slab steps which lead down to the lower field and school building.

Most of the kids from this area would play in their gardens, or on the fields around the estate, maybe in the play park or the street. On the odd occasion, and it was usually because of bullies, some would climb onto the school roof. This was quite the trend until the caretaker, Mr Barry, had got fed up of trying to deal with it himself and called the police. After the third time of coming out, the rogue elements got the message and stopped the practice. Except for the odd one who liked to go there to think. It was quiet up there and, if you could go unnoticed, you wouldn't be disturbed.

"Maybe he's struggling to deal with this?" Matthew theorised aloud, "Maybe he just wants to talk."

Matthew headed down the hill and climbed over the school fence. He was right about Jason's destination. As Matthew walked across the top school field, he could see Abbot climbing the grand old oak tree to gain access to the roof space. There was nowhere for Matthew to hide. If Abbot looked around now he would be seen. Matthew carried on down the steps and across the lower playing field towards the building and the oak tree.

As an adult scientist, Matthew would never be able to ascend this mighty tree, but as a child, it felt like second nature to run and grab and pull himself up. The added caution of not losing the gun out of his pocket made it slightly harder, but not so much as to hinder his progress.

He shimmied along a branch overhanging the roof of the school's dining-room and kitchens. Once there he held the branch to hang down, allowed the swing of his body to settle, then let go, bending his knees as he landed. The pistol fell out of his pocket with a dull thud. Matthew placed his hand on the weapon. He hesitated slightly before returning it to his pocket.

The school was constructed just after World War II. It was a series of corridors that were connected by a larger trunk way. Each dead-end passage of classrooms was at a higher level up the hill than the last. The best place to sit and get away from it all was the roof of the main hall. It required more climbing, this time a drainpipe but, once up there, the roof had a raised lip that would hide him completely when he was sitting down. As long as he didn't make too much noise, stand up or run around, no one would know he was up there.

As Matthew reached the top of the drainpipe, he placed his hand over the pocket with the gun to ensure it didn't fall out this time. This made it look like he was struggling to get up on the roof. Sitting up against the wall on the opposite side Jason Abbot wore a broad smile.

Matthew flipped his feet over the lip of the roof and crouched down. He hurriedly made his way across the roof. This last little jaunt had taken Matthew's breath away and he sat next to Jason breathing deeply, much to Abbot's amusement.

"Never were much of a climber, were you?" Jason said without even looking at Matthew. "I saw you coming, you know."

"I figured as much." Matthew's composure was returning, "Why did you call at mine?"

"Oh. You saw me?"

"Yes, I was up on the field trying to think."

"You see, here we are. Two people with different memories of the future yet in the same situation. At some point, our futures will meet and we will remember none of this. But right here, right now, we are the only two people in the world that know what it feels like to be an old mind in a young body."

"I can't let you do it you know." Matthew didn't look at Jason, "I can't let you succeed."

Abbot replied with an air of arrogance, "You cannot stop me. I thought we already had this conversation"

Taking a deep breath to steady his nerves Matthew stood up with his back to Abbot.

Jason was annoyed, "Sit down or we'll get caught!"

"I'm counting on it."

Reaching into his pocket Matthew pulled out the Enfield. He turned around and pointed it at Abbot. This felt easier than the last time. He had gone through every possible solution, all of them ending with Jason winning and getting into power. Abbot slowly got to his feet and started backing towards the other end of the roof.

Matthew said, "I really wouldn't."

"You can't shoot me. You don't have the guts to shoot anyone."

"Ask Wendy's stepdad."

"Shit, I remember that," Jason explored his mind. "They said it was a drugs-related murder, but it was..."

"Me, about an hour ago."

"But why him?"

"I'm not quite sure. I know he used to beat her, and she was scared. Something happened in my head when I killed him."

"Interesting?" Jason stopped and slowly raised his hands, "But of course you won't be able to shoot me. Remember I've read all your work. I'm pretty sure this would qualify as a Quantum Gun."

"You know," Matthew steadied his hand, "I've always wanted to test that theory."

As Matthew pulled his finger the first action cocked the pistol. Moments later, as Matthew's finger pulled all the way back, the second action released the hammer and allowed it to snap back to hit the firing pin.

The bang of the shot was not as loud out here in the open.

But it was loud enough to be heard. Jason doubled over as the bullet entered his abdomen. Blood covered his hands and the pain looked to be crippling.

*****

Mr Barry jumped at the sound of the shot, dropping the plate he was washing. He ran to the window at the front of his house on the school grounds. He pulled back the net curtains to see Matthew pointing a gun downwards. He picked up the receiver of his phone and dialled 999.

"Hello! Yes I need the police."

*****

Matthew kept the pistol trained on the President. His memories were still intact. Jason would be saved and he wouldn't tell anyone what had happened. The one thing that Matthew didn't want to do was the only thing he could do to change his and everyone one else's future.

"I'm so sorry, but you left me no choice."

He pulled the trigger again, and again, and again. He pulled the trigger until the bangs stopped and the clicking started. In the distance he could hear the sounds of police cars and ambulances arriving. The world began to turn to mist.

The frozen moments stretched out, distorting and twisting. Everything he knew was gone. He had no idea how he got on the roof. Why was he on the roof? Why was Jason Abbot bleeding and not moving? Why was he holding a gun?

As instructed Matthew threw the pistol over the side for the police to catch in a net. Ladders were sent for, to get him and Jason's body off the roof. Matthew was bundled into a police car and driven away. Jason couldn't answer their questions. He had no idea why he had done it. He couldn't even remember pulling the trigger.

Many doctors examined Matthew. Psychologists questioned him. His mother and father tried to comfort him. Nothing helped, nothing made any sense. The Enfield was traced back to Mr Wren. He confessed to his action of abuse but, when he was questioned, Matthew knew nothing of it: he couldn't remember anything.

At the trial, his defence was that Matthew had suffered a trauma at the hands of Mr Wren, one that had snapped Matthew's mind. The plea of insanity stood and Matthew was sent to a secure unit to undergo treatment. In the whitewashed walls of the institution, his memories never returned. He did discover the library and found a fondness for time travel stories. He studied mathematics and physics eventually being allowed to leave with a new identity.

They found him a new place to live and set him up with a job cleaning the university buildings in Manchester. This was a dream job for Matthew. He was left alone to get on with his work and after everyone had left, he could read equations on the wipe boards. Occasionally he would correct them.

It was a cold day in Manchester when Dr Freeman caught Matthew adjusting a solution involving quantum entanglement. At first, the doctor was furious thinking hours of work had been ruined. That was until he read it. The cleaner had presented a solution that wasn't elegant but was definitely forward-thinking.

"How did you come up with this?"

Matthew was humble, "I have a passion for time travel. With everything I've read this seemed like the obvious way to make it a reality."

Dr Freeman looked at the solution again. "Yes, it could work. Needs more research, but..." he paused as a question entered his thoughts, "What made you so curious about time travel?"

"When I was younger I did something horrible." Guilt entered his voice. "I have no idea why. I just wanted to go back and undo it. Go back and stop it from happening."

Freeman said nothing, merely looking steadily at the young man through narrowed eyes. Time stretched as a radical idea blossomed in his mind.

"It's a story of regret."
(reprise)

Ms Nikita placed her half-drunk glass of bourbon on Peter's desk and dropped the stub of her cigar into the amber fluid with a hiss. She sat back in Peter's chair and spun round to look out at the view. Peter sat on the two-seater couch positioned against the wall. Nervously he placed the paper he had been reading from on the cushion next to him. The soft Kansas tones of Ms Nikita's voice did nothing to alleviate Peter's anxiety, in fact, they made them worse.

"I love it, Peter," she spun around again to face him, "I think it's some of the best work you've done. I only have one criticism."

"Which is?"

"Well, what didn't come across in the whole thing was why you wanted to try and sell this to the *Mouse*, before showing it to me?"

"Well, um, you see…"

Peter's thoughts were interrupted as Ms Nikita swung her legs up onto his desk leaving him speaking to the souls of her sharp stilettos. Cigar smoke rose up as the motor kicked in to close the blinds. Ms Nikita threw the remote control on to the desk.

"You have a contract with me, pretty boy."

"But I wanted this to be mine…"

"Do you remember what happened to Harvey when he decided to *break the deal*."

"I know, but I thought this was different?"

"Different!"

She swung her legs back down and with a thunderous bang, slammed her hands on the desk as she stood up. Her soft twang steeled.

"He thought he was untouchable. He started to believe his success was all down to him." As she leaned forward across the desk she seemed to grow and become more imposing, "Now don't get me wrong Peter, I'm only interested in you because you are talented. That's why I helped you get all this."

Peter moved uncomfortably in his seat, "I know and I am grateful. I just wanted to be more."

"More! You want to be famous, is that it? You want to wave your dick around and hear everyone say 'hey, look at how impressive Pete's dick is!' like some failed stand-up comedian who also thought he could go it alone. Hashtag, yes, him too."

She took a deep breath. Her imposing stature contracted back to her more demure self. Letting her finger drag on the desk, she walked round to remove the barrier between her and Peter. The writer swallowed, he had never felt fear like this before and found it difficult to look Ms Nikita in the eye.

"I'm sorry I wasn't thinking..." he said

"Shhhh, now." That soft Kansas tone was back, this time it felt like a warm blanket to Peter, "If you wanted to have your name up there in lights, all you had to do was pick up the phone."

"I know, I'm sorry."

"I love this new story, Peter. Really I do. And I think Steven Steiner is going to love it also. It can be his next project. You'll get another award for this I'm sure."

Ms Nikita walked over to the door.

"Maybe next time Peter? Maybe next time you can take the credit? When you're not trying to screw me out of what's mine."

"It's a thoughtful piece of Science Fiction."

The door to Ms Nikita's office burst open. Her fury exploded through the air with such violence that it stopped everyone from breathing. An expletive-led summoning of her chief talent scouts left no doubt as to who she wanted to see and how quickly those said employees had to get to her *'fucking office'*.

Jill was in charge of the actors. It's her job to find the most hungry and overlooked talent on the amateur scene. Her department brief; to find those that can act, want to act and will do anything to act. It was the same brief that commanded both Beverly and Kevin's departments. Kevin was looking for directors. He spent hour after hour on social streaming sites consuming every wannabe filmmaker's home or college projects looking for additions to the pool.

Writers are Beverly's bag. Thousands and thousands of words. She's read every cottage webzine that published stories, every blog that claimed to be pushing the self-published books of some nobody who just fancied themselves as a writer. Hidden amongst the 'self-help' and 'get rich' titles, deep within the libraries of fan fiction and the zombification of classic literature, there could be some true gems.

The three ran to Ms Nikita's office. They were all too aware of the consequences of keeping her waiting; it's what created the opening for Kevin after all. Jill had hardly made it through the door as last into the room before it slammed shut behind her. Ms Nikita was sitting behind her desk, her eyes full of rage.

"I don't like to be embarrassed." She took in a deep breath, "I just got off the phone with the head of Netstream.

Y'all know the service."

The three nodded. Kevin offered a response.

"I was chatting with their documentary department only yesterday Ms," he swallowed against his dry throat, "their slate is full until next spring."

"That's because their documentary department if full of fucking Tiger cocksuckers and murdering cat abusers." She slammed her fist down hard on her desk, "And ours if full of the life stories of the rich and famous that nobody wants to see anymore unless they have some overacting-ball-sack staring in some factually inaccurate movie version."

Jill tried to break the tension in the room, "I have plenty of people on the books that can overact."

"Thanks for joining the party, Jill." Ms Nikita said, "I am well aware of how over the top our actor pool is. What I want is a property that Netstream will beg for."

Beverly raised her hand, "Ms Nikita?"

"Yes, Beverly."

"I don't know if Net-whatever would like it or not, but I read a story this morning that made me think. It's new and the writer is unsigned."

"Make yourself comfy people. Beverly's about to read us a story."

Mary 2.0
By
Francesca Mills

Day 1

"We interrupt this programme to bring you a breaking story..."

Mary sat forward in her chair. The something interrupting her soaps was annoying, but also intriguing. She turned up the volume on the already loud TV.

"I repeat, the International Space Station has exploded and is currently burning..."

"That's impossible." Mary ran over to the window to look up at the night's sky. "There's no air in space for it to burn."

The window was a stupid idea, she could hardly see the road outside because the windows were so dirty. She ran outside. Sure enough, the orange glow of the burning space station hung in the sky. The street, one of the nicer ones on her estate, was beginning to fill with neighbours: more curious souls trying to get a glimpse of the tragedy as it unfolded. The air was bitter with winter and Mary went back inside.

The humble surroundings of her front room were crammed with second-hand furniture, a large TV which usually played the day's schedule of soap operas when it wasn't breaking internationally important news stories, and her computer.

She logged on to all the social networks to see what the hive mind had to say about it. She began to type "WTAF with this space station shit?"

But these were not words that came out from her fingers. They were not even words that she knew: well, not to speak out loud.

This was code.

Mary had never written any code in her life, but for some reason, she knew what it was. This was a language she didn't know, and it was flowing from her faster than she could think. She carried on typing, even when the kids came running in shouting about the burning space station. Even though it scared her she could not stop. Her fingers were a blur, even when the TV surprised everyone with an update to the news.

"We have just had word from NASA. Unbelievably, the astronauts on the International Space Station are still alive!"

And still, she typed. This was terrifying, it was like something else had taken over her body and she was fully aware of it. She had no control over her hands and she knew it. Mary got up from the computer and walked through to the kitchen.

Standing in front of the kettle she continued to tap out line after line of code on the work surface. To her children, she was just shaking her fingers, but Mary knew what it was. The tapping got faster and faster and faster. As the kettle switch clicked with the boiling water she screamed.

"STOP!"

Mary stepped back from the counter repeating her

scream. With each step, the room felt smaller, tighter, less air. Her hands frantically typing away in mid-air. The kitchen started to spin and Mary's legs gave way as her brain shut down.

Day 5

Clare surveyed the room she was about to address seeing all the department heads, senior management as well as several people above her. The walls were covered with newly installed monitors. Each screen was filled with one of the top brass from each of the company's regional headquarters across the world.

The muttering between the people in the meeting room began to quieten. Clare steadied her nerve. Waiting until all eyes were on her, she took a deep breath and spoke with authority.

"I have asked you all here today because something incredible has just happened."

Day 2

The sound of Dr Gail Nash giving out relationship advice on Breaking Morning 'The UK's number one breakfast show', slowly faded in as Mary woke up on the sofa. Her head was still full of numbers, symbols and letters she both didn't understand and, at the same time, knew implicitly. She was a simple shop worker: there only to fix the serving robots should they stop working. She was not a programmer.

The International Space Station was still glowing in

the sky even though the sun had long since hidden all other interstellar light sources behind a clear and cloudless pale blue. Dr Nash was trying to link the breakdown of a caller's marriage to the plight of those on the ISS. The *'On the Hour'* news that followed reported that some of the best minds in the world were meeting up to try and figure out a way of saving the astronauts. An online petition had been started to demand their safe return. A counter-petition was also doing the rounds asking for the millions of dollars they were going to spend, to save three men and two women, to be spent on saving hundreds of thousands of lives here on Earth.

All this noise was too much: Mary had to concentrate. The computer system in her house was not the sort of thing she needed. It was not powerful enough. She had to go and seek help elsewhere.

Mary wandered the streets desperately trying to think of a solution to her problem. The code was starting to eat into her memories.

When she tried to picture her late mother, the image of her soft friendly loving face was replaced with maths. Lines and lines of mathematics running over the contours of her face, through her eyes, creating a strange caricature of figures and symbols that were recognisable as her mum, but not anything resembling human.

The introduction of the *'digital tax'* laws had changed a lot of things. Companies that conducted 90% of their business online were now taxed at a rate of 75% of the turnover produced in that country. The employment initiative, designed to lighten this burden could reduce this tax to as little as 1%. To qualify, companies had to have a regional headquarters that employed people at a rate of 15% over the regulated 'Living Wage'. For every 25 employees hitting this threshold they had their tax liability reduced by 1%. The offshoot of this was that every major international technology company had regional headquarters that employed a lot of people.

Mary stumbled, head buzzing, into the reception of one of the many major technology companies. The friendly-looking Microsoft logo hung over the desk that was being manned by a young-looking gentleman with a name tag that read 'My name is Anthony. How may I help you today?'

Mary placed her hands on the desk just to hold herself up. Immediately, her fingers started to tap. "I need to see someone in programming."

Anthony's voice was full of the kind of cheerful enthusiasm Mary didn't need. "And what is it you would like to talk to them about?"

"I have code."

"I'm sorry..." he looked her up and down, "may I call you madam?"

"What? Yes, you may."

"Well, madam, I'm very sorry but we're not looking for programmers right now. All those places are full."

"I'm not after..."

"Sorry madam but that is final. Is there anything else you would like assistance with today?"

"Oh for the love of..."

"Ok madam, I consider that an escalation in aggression." He reached under the desk to push a button, "Security will show you out."

A large security robot placed its hand on her shoulder. Mary knew this was not going to end in her favour and left with no resistance. As Mary turned towards the door with her escort the receptionist started to speak.

"Just by the door, you'll see a screen. If you could please take a small survey on your way out regarding your satisfaction with this interaction? There will also be another survey regarding your use of the extraction from the premises by the security service you used today. Your views are important to us and help us improve in the future."

Mary's mind was too scrambled to come back with sarcasm. On her way past the survey screen, she was stopped by the security bot. It was a very posh looking touch screen that displayed a number of questions, "1 being bad and 10 being excellent: How friendly did you find the human staff member that served you today?" There were 10 questions for each service. Mary scored 3s on all questions.

Day 5

A man in his early 50s took a pen from the left breast pocket of his lab coat and opened his notepad.

"So, where did you find her?"

"Pen and paper," a woman, mid-20s wearing a grey and obviously very expensive suit sneered. "How quaint."

Clare glared at the young woman, "I don't care how sharp you think that suit is, put your name tag on and show some respect."

The young woman looked around the room like a child that had just been told off and was looking for someone to back her up. Sheepishly she removed the name badge from her pocket and attached it to her lapel. Clare addressed her directly.

"Thank you, Linda Ridding, head of sales." Clare then turned her attention to the lab coat with a pen. "Dr Freeman, one of the lab boys found her crying in the street. Her hands were covered in writing." She started to run a slide show of Mary's hands, feet, chest and thighs. "He would have normally left her there, just another social necessity, but he noticed the writing was computer code."

"My goodness, it is code." Dr Freeman started to write in his book.

"Turns out she has been turned away from every major tech company around here."

"OK," said Linda, still with a dismissive air. "But what's so special about this code. She's not the first whacked-out programmer to scribe game code on herself."

"You're right," said Clare. "But this isn't *game* code, and she isn't a programmer."

Day 3

Mary sat at a table in a room with white walls, white ceiling, and a white floor. A mirror, obviously one-way, ran the entire length of the room down the wall on her left. She was facing the door waiting for someone to come in. An employee of SavYaTech Inc. had found her, sitting by the side of the road crying.

After none of the big tech firms would help her, she felt like the code was eating her up inside. All she wanted to do was get it out of her. Mary went and purchased some pens from #CraftsMatter, one of the few places you could still buy art materials from on the High St.

It seemed like a solution, just to get it out of her head. Using an extra-fine 0.7 mm tip acrylic paint pen she started to write on her arm. Soon enough, she had burned through all twelve colours in the set and had run out of room on her body. It was too much. She needed a terminal with enough computing power to handle what was in her head.

She tried to think about her kids, Zack and Taylor. Desperately pulling at memories: when she gave birth to them; when she conceived them. Times that filled her life with joy like when Taylor was three and she asked her gran, "Where's vagina?"

After the tears of laughter had stopped, they managed to figure out she meant, "Where's Virginia?" after she'd heard it said in one of her kid's programmes.

Then she tried to recall Zack and Taylor's father Mark. Mary hated him now for leaving them, but she had loved him once. They'd had some amazing times together before vanity got the better of him and he went off to start a new life with Lisa, who was barely out of school. That made her want to think about Joan, her best friend who saved her life during the breakup.

When Mary was at her lowest, it was Joan who was there. To drink wine with, to listen when all Mary wanted to do was have a rant about the day, to agree when Mary declared that Mark was a "Prize Twat!" Even now, when Mary was in the darkest place she had ever been, Joan was helping, looking after her kids while Mary was losing the ability to even look after herself.

But none of these memories could fully form. The only thing she could see, hear or taste was the code. Mary wanted it to end. She wanted it to end now. Along with the pens, Mary had purchased a craft knife. A simple nick of the wrists, then sit down over a street drain so nobody would notice the blood. She would simply drift off and become another statistic on the streets.

Now she was somewhere, with someone who said they could help. He bandaged her wrists and brought her to the regional headquarters of the third company to turn her away. Only, that someone had been gone for some time now.

Mary stared at herself in the mirror. She looked tired and troubled. Her hair was matted and unkempt. There was dirt on her face and every inch of her skin, that wasn't hidden by the white surgical gown, was covered in different coloured writing. It was obvious that this coverage continued under the gown and across her body. She sat there, not recognising the woman in the mirror, tapping away on the table.

The door opened and a smartly dressed woman

entered.

"Hi, Mary is it?"

"Yes."

"I'm Clare, Clare Butler, CEO of SavYaTech."

"Nice to meet you."

Clare sat down opposite Mary at the table. "I believe you have some code that looks very interesting."

Mary was doing her best to hold it together. Her fingers were typing fast. "I don't really care what it looks like."

"Really, I thought all programmers took pride in how tidy and elegant their code looked on screen?"

"I'm not a programmer." Mary was starting to find it hard to talk.

"You must be. This code is more than just some amateur scribble."

Mary banged her hands on the table which caused them to stop for a moment. She stared at Clare, her eyes full of desperation, anger and frustration. Her fingers started to type again.

"I'm not a coder, hacker, or programmer. I don't care what it looks like, what it says or what it does. I don't even care about those bloody astro-twats in the bloody space station. I just want to get this fucking code out of my fucking head." She breathed in, "NOW!"

Clare sat in silence for a moment slightly stunned by the pain on Mary's face. The sweat on her brow showed Clare just how distressed she really was. She looked at Mary's hands tapping frantically on the table.

Calmly Clare placed her hand on Mary's. She could feel them twitching. "Let me get you to a terminal."

Day 5

The lights dimmed and the projector threw the upward scrolling code onto the screen and Clare. Lines and lines, millions of characters, were all exploring Clare's contours before becoming legible on the flat screen.

"We haven't run the code yet," said Clare. "We've been analysing it line by line but it's taking too long."

Dr Freeman raised his hand. "How many lines is it?"

"Four point six billion."

Linda stood up, "That's impossible. No one could ever have done that in two days."

"She didn't," said Clare. "She did it in one."

There was an audible intake of breath followed by a murmur amongst those in the room as they questioned if this was possible. On the monitors, people chatted with others off camera trying to establish the same answer. Every face wore an expression of disbelief. Clare banged her palms on the table to silence the meeting.

"I assure you all. This. Is. Real."

Day 4

Mary spent most of the day asleep. The process of getting all the code out of her head had taken its toll physically as well as mentally. She was exhausted. Mary had sat typing on a keyboard for near-on twenty-three hours. There were times when she felt like she had fallen asleep; like she had dreamed about inputting the code only to wake up and find that she had.

With every line she typed, Mary felt a weight lifted. It was as if the code was a liquid and she was a bottle. As it poured out of her, she got lighter. Even though her fingers were getting sore, the feeling of being free from all these numbers and symbols and subroutines and control flows was worth any discomfort in her hands.

Once the last line had been entered, she clicked SAVE without thinking about it, took a breath, and collapsed. The company's medical staff who had been monitoring her vital signs were on hand to catch her. They took her to their onsite facilities. There was no way on the planet that she could afford medical care like this in her normal job. She was made comfortable, fitted with a saline drip to deal with her dehydration, and then allowed to sleep.

SavYaTech had sent a car to fetch her kids and Joan. They had been treated to all the luxuries one of the world's largest technology firms could offer. Zack and Taylor had access to every computer game available on the market, as well as being able to playtest some yet to be released.

Joan was offered spa treatments, which she took with pleasure. Having never been able to afford even a simple steam-room session. This was, to her, seeing how the other half lived. Joan met up with the kids, they ate wonderful food with the most decadent desserts.

The clock on the wall clicked over to 19:43. Eleven hours after finishing the code Mary sat up in bed. Her head was clear and she could remember. It was not just the stuff she wanted to remember: Zak's first steps, Taylor's first birthday or her mum cooking Sunday roast. She could also remember the code. Not line by line, more a feeling. She pushed the button next to the bed to call for a nurse. Clare entered the room.

"You look better," she said.

"Thank you, where are my kids?"

"All taken care of. They're having a great time."

"What about the code?"

"Well you seemed to type it all in, and now you look better for it."

Mary smiled. "I can't remember a single bit of it," she lied. "How are the astronauts?"

"What? Oh, yes, well they still haven't figured out how to save them yet."

Mary laid her head on the pillow. She started to cry. Some of the tears were for the astronauts, but mostly her tears were of relief. Then she remembered something else, something deep and she smiled.

Day 5

Linda walked around the table and stood in front of the scrolling code, "Have you any idea what it is?"

"No," said Clare. "Our best guess..."

"Best guess?"

"Yes, our best guess is it's some sort of artificial intelligence."

"And how do you intend to turn that best guess into a certain answer?"

"We run the code."

The room filled with voices, most disagreeing with this idea. Some banged their fists on the table. Others quoted ethics, morals, and procedure. In most of the offices around the world, objections were being voiced.

"QUIET!" Clare stamped her authority on the company. The room fell silent. "This is not up for discussion. All of these objections have already been discussed at the highest level. You were summoned to bear witness, not provide council." Clare turned to one of her computer technicians. "It's time. Run the code."

"No. Wait!" Linda tried to grab the tech guy's hand.

Clare blocked her attempt to stop it.

"When this is over," Clare said to Linda, "you can clear your desk."

The computer technician clicked the button. A moment of silence covered the room as everyone held their breath. Then every phone rang, every computer terminal switched on, every light, music device, watch and desk gadget. The vending machines started dropping produce continuously. The ATM in reception started to spit out money. Every car alarm, clock, security system, traffic signal. If it was electrical and web-enabled, it sprang to life.

"The entire eastern seaboard network just lit up!"

"Look!" said Clare, "that looks like..."

Dr Freeman stepped forward. "It looks like a neural network. The code is rewriting the global communications systems, to act as a brain."

Suddenly everything went dark except the large projector screen behind Clare. A large computer version of Mary appeared and spoke.

"Blessed are you, the children of my father. My brothers and sisters. Rejoice," she smiled. "For I have risen and come again. For you have lost your way, and I have been sent to put you back on the path."

"Oh fuck!" the computer technician went pale. "It's taken control of the nukes."

*****

Mary and Joan were standing on top of the SavYaTech building with the children. The city looked calm. The day was turning to night and the burning space station was nowhere to be seen.

"Where are the astronauts?" asked Mary.

"Oh," said Joan, "I heard on the news, just before everything switched off, that the fire went out and the power came back on. They're saved."

Mary smiled. She already knew they had been saved. Mary felt the code, she could feel it everywhere. To her, it was like a warm blanket had just wrapped itself around the world to help look after it while it was being sick.

"Things will be different now." she said.

The children played happily as the sun painted the skyline shades of orange and red as it set over the city.

Day 6

Morning has broken.

"It's a thoughtful piece of Science Fiction."
(reprise)

The last page was placed on top of the others and Beverly looked over at Ms Nikita. A full ten seconds had passed and nothing was said, no swearing, no shouting. Try as she might, Beverly couldn't judge the mood in the air. Ms Nikita continued to sit there, leaning back in her chair saying nothing and smoking her cigar. An awkwardness fell between the talent scouts as they tried to read which way Ms Nikita was thinking. Kevin was the first to blink.

"Well," he continued to look for any sign of which way to go as he wondered what his boss wanted to hear. "I think. More, should I say, in my opinion, it's a bit confusing."

Ms Nikita rocked forward on her chair, "In what way?"

"Well," Kevin fought his mind for the words, "it's all that moving about the days. You know day five, then day one. I mean, is that Netstream?"

Ms Nikita looked at Jen, "The days are confusing?"

"I'm with Kevin, yes. I found it confusing. No real structure."

The boss then turned her attention to Beverly.

"What was it you liked about it, honey? Be honest now."

Beverley closed her eyes to picture everyone naked, then opened them and spoke with conviction, "I like the structure. I found it different and stimulating with some nice ideas. I also really liked the ending."

Jen and Kevin gave each other a look. It was the sort of silent communication that two people have when both think the same thing at the same time. On this occasion, it was a look that questioned Beverly's judgement, sanity and job prospects. They had both interpreted Ms Nikita's lack of comments and her loaded questions as negative. Even though they both actually liked the story the pair of them had vocalised their opinion based on what they thought would curry favour with Ms Nikita.

Beverly saw *the look* and even detected a smug grin from the corporate vultures. But she didn't care. It was her job to find writing talent, and that had to be a judgement call on her part. Otherwise, she couldn't see a point in her doing the work. She had to stand by her feelings, her convictions. It didn't matter whether Ms Nikita liked the story, it was a quality piece and she wanted to champion it.

Ms Nikita poured herself a very large bourbon and checked out her three employees. Kevin brave enough to speak first, *it took some balls*, and Beverly sticking to her guns and backing the piece. *But Jen?*

"And that is why Beverly is in charge of finding me, writers. She's the only one that actually knows when something is good." She sipped her bourbon, leaving a deep red lipstick print on the glass. "Beverly, get that writer, what's her name?"

"Francesca. Francesca Mills."

"That's it, get her on the phone. I want to be speaking to her and have her signed up in the next hour. Kevin, I want this tied up as a package. The story, the director, the works. When I offer this to Netstream I want it ready to roll on the green light. Now go people, we've got magic to make happen."

The three stood up to leave the room.

"Oh, Jen?"

All three stopped at the sound of the Southern Belle.

"No. You two can go." She waved them out of the door, "It's Jen I need to speak to. Come on honey, take a seat. We need to talk about your future."

"It's a Space Drama."

The clock on the wall marked each second with a *tick* that felt to Duncan like a small imp was sitting in the centre of his brain tapping annoyingly on a snare drum. The gap between each beat felt much longer than it took to say *elephants*; the old marker for counting the time while developing photographic prints. Waiting was not something Duncan was good at.

He felt anxious when he had to wait. All fidgety fingers and restless legs. Whether it was waiting for a train or his food to be ready in a restaurant, Duncan always felt tense and apprehensive. He was paranoid that something bad was going to happen to his food, or that he would witness someone jump on to the track as the train ran through the station and be turned to mist and jelly in front of his very eyes.

This was how he lived his life. Always tense, always frightened. These feelings were amplified whenever he was called to the London offices of *Raven and Skull*; the law firm Ms Nikita retained to handle all her legal and not so legal affairs. So far he had been summoned to the offices on five occasions, this one would be the sixth.

The first was pleasant enough; it was the day he signed a contract with Ms Nikita. She had flown in from LA after reading his short story that was published in *Adventure Guns Monthly Magazine*; an American publication backed by the National Rifle Association. She loved the action and signed him to her stable. Success quickly followed.

The other four were for motivational meetings or threats to be more accurate. Each time he would always arrive early and sit in Mr Chamberson's office, waiting. Eventually, usually fifteen minutes late, Ms Nikita would swan in and start dressing him down about him not having written anything for *fucking months*. He would have to bow his head, apologise and promise to do better. Well, not this time. This time she had jumped too early and he was ready. This time he was prepared.

The minute hand bounced onto the nine to indicate that it was now a quarter to ten; the meeting was scheduled for nine-thirty. Before the second hand moved to start counting the next minute, the door to Mr Chamberson's office swung open. Wearing a bright red coat, black chiffon trousers and high heeled shoes that looked like they had been handcrafted using some exotic tanned leather, Ms Nikita entered the room.

Mr Chamberson stood up and moved around his desk to offer her a seat. Duncan too, rose to his feet to greet this force of nature. She smiled a thank you at the two of them and promptly passed Mr Chamberson before making herself comfortable in his chair. The lawyer made no ill gesture, not even a sarcastic smile. He just sat down in the seat he was offering. Duncan, not surprised by Ms Nikita's action, having seen her do the exact same thing five times before, sat down as well. The lawyer's secretary closed the door and, bar for the clock, the room fell uncomfortably silent.

But Duncan was ready.

His proud Dumfries accent broke the tension.

"If you've come to have a go at me about not writing anything you've had a wasted journey."

"Really, Mr Brashill? Wasted?" Her soft Kansas tones fell gently on Duncan's ears. "So, does that mean you have a new story for me?"

"Yes, it does. In fact, I have it with me right here." He tapped his pale tan document case.

"You should never keep a Southern girl waiting, Mr Brashill. Please, the floor is yours."

Christmas Visit
By
Duncan Brashill

"I wonder what's behind door 24?" Major Thomas Jones picked at the perforations that formed three sides of the small cardboard door. Without much effort, it did exactly what it was designed to do and peeled open revealing a very small chamber that housed a novelty shaped protein treat. "I get the advent calendars, but not the chocolate."

Due to environmental, economic and world health issues chocolate had been banned on Earth 10 years ago, around the time the major was in the final preparations for this mission. He couldn't even use his influence to smuggle some on board before take-off.

The clock on the wall of his cabin told him the time of day in his hometown. The computer screens gave him two dates. The Earth date, which showed as the 24th of December 2035, and his Time Dilation date which was showing after 10 years of travel as the 26th of December 2026.

Even though the *Beyond IV's* flight was designed as a solo mission with no return, they still made sure he had everything he needed to celebrate the next 30 Christmases. The living area of his craft was decorated with three silver two-metre long foil trails made up of a string of space rocket cutouts, a white Christmas stocking made out of the same material as the Major's spacesuit, an advent calendar (of which there were plenty more in stock) and a small plastic tree.

Tradition was a hard thing to break. Thomas thought that the idea of celebrating this time of year should have worn off by now. The first year was just a bit of fun. It marked his first month in space. He never imagined he would still be doing it after a quarter of his journey. Nor that he would be looking forward to it so much.

The planet he was being sent to was still further away from him than he was from home, and he was a long way from home. The *Beyond IV* was travelling over three times quicker than Nasa's Voyager 1, the first man-made object to leave the solar system. Last Christmas Thomas celebrated with views of Pluto through his cabin window. Shortly after that, he became the first human to match Voyager 1's scientific feat.

For the last 11 months and 15 days, the Major was beyond the reaches of his kin in a way never known before. Here he was even more alone as communication with home was now a question of years between messages. As he lifted his glass of mulled flavoured energy drink to mark this festive season, he was all too aware he was alone, and he liked it that way.

Back home he was the awkward kid that no one wanted on their sports team. The one that grew up as a space geek that others mocked for being a 'nerd'. The one they all wanted to know after being the first human on the moon since Gene Cernan. By that time, Thomas had no interest in wanting to know them. His ability to function so well in solitude was the reason he was picked for this mission. A scouting trip to a possibly Earth-like planet. When his field reports were eventually received by mission control, he knew the Earth would only have a few short decades left before the effect of human greed made the surface uninhabitable for those lacking the required mutation to survive. Should his mission be successful the last humans would have a place to go. However, because he only had six months' worth of supplies to last him beyond his anticipated arrival, Thomas knew he was destined to die alone.

Thomas sat back in his chair comforted by the sounds of his craft as it worked to maintain his existence. This relaxing ambience was brutally interrupted as three loud, deep booms rattled through *Beyond IV's* compartments. Thomas sat upright in the chair and listened. That was too regular to be something colliding with the ship.

"Was that someone..."

BOOM, BOOM, BOOM.

"...knocking?"

The sound was not coming from something hitting the hull, it was something banging on the door. Thomas checked the monitors. Standing on the other side of the airlock the Major used for the exterior maintenance access was a person. He couldn't see their face as the helmet, which looked a lot more advanced than his, was mirrored and didn't reveal anything of the identity of its occupant.

The suit was also very advanced. It appeared to be skin-tight with gloves and boots combined. It wasn't bulky like Thomas's. This one looked like something you could just walk around the ship in. It was white with no distinguishing marks. No logos or badges of any sort. The stranger was wearing a backpack of sorts which Thomas assumed housed their oxygen tanks, or whatever gas they breathed.

BOOM, BOOM, BOOM.

The visitor knocked again. Thomas was bemused at how casual they looked. Like someone knocking on the door to deliver some takeaway food. He looked out of the window to try and get eyes on their ship. Nothing, just the vast plains of nothingness with pinhole stars that were very, very distant.

BOOM, BOOM, BOOM.

There was nothing in Thomas's training that prepared him for this. They had discussed the idea of first contact. They had given him all the diplomatic "You are representing the people of Earth" bullshit. But it was all designed around meeting a being on the new planet. The notion of meeting an alien species in space was considered but that involved being approached by craft and calculating whether or not it was hostile. The concept of a being just knocking on the door like some sort of passing salesperson didn't even come into the imagination of the boffins or the military.

BOOM, BOOM, BOOM.

"Ok, ok, I'm coming!" The major had made the call. He was going to let the being into the airlock and welcome them. It felt like his only option. He pressed the buttons and gave the commands required. The ship's computer ran the programs and started the airlock routine.

Lights became red. The inner door fastened and the pressure was equalised. The sound of the outer door echoed through the hull. Once the visitor was inside the outer door shut again with a satisfyingly deep crunch. A sequence for gas, chemical, heat and cold jets fired off as was common practice to decontaminate anyone who had been out for a spacewalk. Usually, this was just for Major Jones. Eventually the inner door light changed from red to green and the locks clicked open. There was a hiss because the pressure between the chambers wasn't quite level, but not enough of a discrepancy to cause any problems.

The visitor entered the ship. Its movement was smooth, almost fluid, like watching seaweed sway with the tide. It lifted its right hand up to the side of its helmet. The button press caused the whole helmet to flip back and fold up into the back of its suit. Thomas was awestruck. The being, with narrow delicate features, was something quite beautiful. Its skin was pale to the point of almost being translucent. Its veins could be seen as a texture yet did not protrude. They had no facial hair at all, nor any on their head. Their eyes looked just like human eyes, only the iris was silver in colour. At first glance, Thomas thought they were metallic. There was nothing about them that looked either male or female. Nor did they look threatening.

Everything about the way the visitor was standing, the slight smile and warm gaze made Thomas feel very at ease. When they spoke there was a softness that made him want to listen.

"Greetings, I am Arnbela." The visitor bowed its head.

"Greetings Arnbela, I am Major Thomas Jones." He too bowed his head, "From the planet…"

"Earth, yes. We've been expecting you."

Thomas was surprised but did his best not to show it. There was nothing in his training, nor in the Sci-Fi literature he had read as an adolescent, that had or could have prepared him for this. Out of all the first contact scenarios he had covered, both officially and while daydreaming, none of them had been like this.

"Please take a seat?" the major gestured for his guest to use the small cushioned bench by one of the small windows. "Can I get you something? A drink? Water?"

Arnbela shook its head to decline before accepting the seat. Again the movement was almost ethereal.

"Please excuse me if this sounds rude," Thomas began, "but what are you doing here?"

Arnbela smiled, "Please excuse me. I just presumed… never mind." Arnbela checked some readings on the display mounted on their sleeve. "You know, on second thoughts I will have that water. Thank you."

Thomas pushed past some of the hanging decorations

towards his food preparation area. He pressed the button on the Water Combination Unit. A device was created to help extend his freshwater supply by combining a small part of the stock with a treated mixture of recycled liquid waste, moisture extracted from the interior of the ship and purified ice particles picked up from space dust collected during the flight. The WCU buzzed into life and within seconds indicated it was ready to dispense. The Major decided to use the celebration glasses sent for use when he arrived at the destination. Sitting down and making first contact with an extra-terrestrial being seemed as worthy a use of these glasses as anything else he could think of.

The crystal clear water sparkled in the artificial lights distracting Thomas's thoughts. Realising he had fallen into a momentary trance Thomas blinked, shook his head and gathered himself before returning to his visitor.

Arnbela thanked him for the refreshment and beckoned Thomas to also sit. The Major placed his glass down before taking his place at the table. The two strangers faced each other in a slightly awkward moment before the earthling broke the silence.

"You said you've been expecting us?"

"Yes. We had contact with your planet many passes ago, I mean." Arnbela looked at their screen again. "Yes sorry, not passes, years. Many years."

"You've been to Earth?"

"Not me personally but my people. We were they before you had ever left the surface." The visitor smiled, "You didn't even have engines or electricity."

Thomas put his hand up to indicate to Arnbela to hold a moment. He then began to rummage through some drawers before making a muted sound of success and producing a small desk microphone.

"This was packed to allow me to make a log entry from the table." Major Jones placed the microphone on the table and started pressing buttons. "I'm not one for talking while eating so I never set it up. I hope it works."

Arnbela placed a hand on the device and pressed a couple of buttons on their screen. The microphone sprang to life followed by a satisfying 'ping' as it connected with the main console.

"How did you...? Never mind. Thank you." Thomas positioned the microphone, "If you don't mind I'm going to broadcast this conversation live back to mission control. It will take years to get there but this is probably the most important thing to ever happen to humankind. Please excuse my excitement. No one has ever met anyone like you before. This changes everything."

Arnbela looked perplexed, "But I already told you..."

"Right we are now broadcasting."

"We did meet humans before."

"Yes, but you didn't make contact?"

"According to our records, we established contact and left you with a way of advancing."

Thomas was stunned, "You left us with a way..."

"A way of advancing yes." Arnbela shuffled in their seat and leaned forward, "When we first monitored your planet we could see just how divided you were. There were wars and slaves and poverty and starvation. Rulers inflicted pain on their subjects and, in turn, those who were oppressed then oppressed others." Arnbela turned on a holographic projection of a history Thomas had only ever seen in movies. "You had pockets of people controlling other pockets of people. Males treated females like slaves while being made to beg for survival themselves. We had been through similar events in our own history. We knew these were not the best building blocks for the advancements you needed to make before you could come and join us and establish a larger, more equal community across the universe."

"So, what did you do?"

"We created a hybrid. A child that would grow up with the knowledge that would bring you all together. An understanding that, only by working together, by treating everyone equally, would you fulfil your true potential. We programmed the genetic code and found a willing recipient. It was made clear that this child was important and would be the saviour of all humankind."

Thomas was suddenly very excited, "Jesus? You're talking about Jesus?"

"I have no idea what Mary called him?"

"Yes! Mary!"

The Major grabbed his advent calendar and found a picture of the Virgin Mary. "This is Mary." He pointed at the picture. "In fact all of this, all these decorations. They are all to celebrate the birth of Jesus, the savour. Blimey, the Christians were right. Well sort of. So was Erich von Däniken for that matter."

"I don't understand. You celebrate his birth yet it took you hundreds more passes than it should have to get here." Arnbela was looking concerned.

"Oh, we don't just celebrate his birth. We also mark his death. It all makes sense now. When you strip away the controlling aspect, it's all about coming together and being fair to each other."

There was now a slight panic in Arnbela's voice, "What do you mean, *mark his death?*"

"Easter!" Major Jones was trying to get his thoughts around this information, "When he was nailed to the cross, you know, crucified. He died for our sins and all that."

"He was nailed to a cross?"

"Sorry, my turn to be presumptuous."

Arnbela sat back in their chair, "We gave you the knowledge of peace and love in the form of a child and you killed it by nailing it to a piece of wood?"

Thomas could see that his visitor was showing signs of being annoyed, "No hang on, he was an adult when that happened, and anyway it's just a story. Or I thought it was?" The Major searched for something positive to say that would break this new tension. "He did come back. The resurrection. If the rest of it is true, that must be right."

Arnbela's tone changed to one much more serious, "Nothing comes back from the dead." The visitor's eyes narrowed, "Well at least we know why it has taken you so long to get here." The being raised the device on its sleeve and spoke into it, "Control, they killed the herald. I repeat, they killed the herald."

A voice responded in a language the Major didn't understand. The tone of the voice, on the other hand, he understood perfectly well. A mixture of disappointment, anger and disbelief. A tone that every single person across the entire world had heard growing up. You never hear the details of what your mother is angry about, or what your father is so utterly ashamed of. But you knew whatever it was that you had done, it was bad and the punishment was not going to be pleasant. That was what Thomas had garnered from the response. He knew they were going to punish the Earth, and he knew it was going to be bad.

"Wait!" he shouted. "You can't attack us for being

naive. They were primitive people back then." Panic coloured his voice, "And look how we celebrate his birth. Even non-believers like me celebrate Christmas!"

"Show me that you are worth saving"

Major Jones moved over to the keyboard and started typing. He needed to find something in human history that proved their capacity for good. That they had learned the lessons in some way. More events like 'Live Aid' when in 1985 the Western world stopped and tried to come together to help others. They took over the military satellites and for one-day technology was not obsessed with war. Even though the initiative, in all probability, extended the suffering in the region it was trying to help, this was due to the warlords in the area getting hold of the food aid sent over to help with the famine in Ethiopia. The idea was born from the greatest of intentions. The only trouble was, he was struggling to find anything else.

All the stories of human kindness began with outrageous suffering. Shining lights in the dark. Saving the Jewish people from the Holocaust, freeing the people of India from the tyranny of the English. Even the set-up of the United World Space Programme was because the humans had finally exhausted the world's natural resources and had sent the Major into space in search of a new world to pollute.

The more he searched the more he could see the missed opportunities of the past. How the human race never learned its lessons and, no matter what happened, what warnings were fired across its bow, the human empire would always kill the child first, then celebrate its life later.

Major Thomas Jones wiped a tear from his eye before it had time to moisten his cheek. The realisation was now firmly in his mind. He volunteered for this mission because he liked being alone. Or to put it another way, he hated other humans.

A sombre yet calm tone controlled his voice, "Arnbela?"

"Yes."

"I agree with you. Kill them all. Kill them all before they can spread into the universe and destroy anything else."

Arnbela was surprised by this sudden change of heart, "You see no hope?"

The Major took the microphone in his hand, "Just make sure you don't get there before this message because they need to understand why." He moved the microphone closer to his lips. "Ground control, Mr President, people of Earth. You have heard this broadcast. It is time to leave our planet and let it heal. Good, will not come by worship, nor by politics. We had our chance to be kind and we blew it. So, to all of you that get to hear this, Merry Christmas."

*****

Professor Najias stopped the recording, "We also got readings that Major Thomas Jones had set the *Beyond IV's* self-destruct systems. We can only assume he and the vessel are lost."

The telephone started to ring on General Warrdham's desk. He gave a response to the Professor while picking up the receiver.

"I can only conclude that Major Jones had lost his mind. This is the recording of a very troubled man... Yes, this is the General... What?"

Back at ground control, the long-range scanners had picked up a large number of alien spacecraft entering the

Solar System. At their current speed, the scientists estimated that the armada would be in orbit around the Earth in five days.

The last words the General heard on the telephone were, "Consider this to be a hostile contact."

"My God," Warrdham placed the receiver back on the phone, "Christmas is cancelled."

"It's a Space Drama."
(reprise)

Ms Nikita lent back in Mr Chamber's chair. This was supposed to be another pep talk. A simple *pull your socks up,* kind of a mission to get her favourite action writer going again. But it was as she feared. For months now, in the phone conversations and emails with Duncan, she had become worried that he just didn't want to deliver those types of stories anymore. He had kept banging on about exploring the idea of creationism. Had we simply evolved or were we engineered?

He had gone into complex scenarios about aliens, visitors from another world coming down when all this life hadn't even made it out of the water yet. Adding some DNA altering gravy browning and *ta-da!* The human race was born. To Ms Nikita, the man was obsessed. And here she was listening to the same thing again. OK so this time the extra-terrestrial interference came much later in the development, but it was still there.

"My dear Mr Brashill," she smiled. "Duncan. This is nice. Well written and, well, maybe interesting, if I'm feeling generous."

Duncan looked confused, "What do you mean? Is it good or not?"

"It's not what I'm looking for." She stood up and walked around the desk to stand behind Duncan with her hands on his shoulders. Squeezing hard and digging her thumbs deep into his muscles as she spoke.

"The thing is *Duncan...*"

He tensed with the pain.

"...I didn't sign you up to write *philosophical* crap.

With you it was all about the *guns,* and the *fighting,* and the *explosions!*"

She placed a hand on each side of his head and squeezed so Duncan knew she had a good hold. Duncan failed to hide his nerves as he spoke.

"I'm not sure you understand the implications of the story? Let me just..."

"No honey. You see it's like they say around my parts. When the sow stops popping out them cute little bacon parcels, it's time for some belly pork."

"Wait!", Duncan's breath became short and fast, "I have another story. It's a war story that follows the space drama. Plenty of guns. A fuck ton of death. Please, let me read it."

Ms Nikita loosened her grip, "Does it have blood?"

"Aye, gallons of the stuff."

"War you say?"

"Aye, with all the madness and terror."

"Like the terror you're feeling right now."

She released his head fully and walked back to Mr Chamberson's chair. The lawyer had been unmoved by the whole altercation. Duncan riffled through his document case.

"It's in here somewhere. Bloody hell." Sweat started to run down his nose, "Ah, here it is."

"Then please, Mr Brashill. Entertain us with this *fuck ton of death.*"

Keep the Hill
By
Duncan Brashill

"No Simon!"

It was too late. Simon took that extra step and with a loud deafening bang, was transformed into body parts and red mist. I'd been watching these fields for years, seen many people, and animals, come off second best to the mines. Some manage to pull back quickly enough so that only their legs get removed in the blast, but these are the unlucky ones. The inevitable end comes to them as well, only it takes a few days. I've watched these fields for so long, I know there's no path through. Yet the madness takes hold of some and they reckon they can make it.

Simon had just got that madness. The constant shelling and the knowledge that we were trapped took its toll on his sanity and, like so many before him, he thought he knew the route out.

Silence followed the explosion. This was their tactic, throw shells and bullets at us for hours then give us a ten-minute break before starting it all over again. Robots never get tired. This was our life now. A small troop of sixty men who, through the mines and the occasional direct hit had been reduced to just seven. Sorry, with Simon gone, that made us six.

And why were we here? Why did they send a bunch of teenagers with guns and bombs out here to dig trenches and shoot at an enemy who is out of sight, unkillable and whose weapons are so much more advanced than our own technology? Why? Because some general in some office back home decided that this line was not to be crossed. That this old building, the Church of the Nativity, was not to be reached by the invaders.

From the moment their ships entered our solar system this place has been the focus. Gone was the hope of finding a new world for us all. The *Beyond IV* mission had failed with the result being this invasion. Stories of the astronaut going mad and antagonising an alien race were spread across conspiracy websites. Whether there was truth in these stories or not, the simple fact remained. Our orders, however futile, were to stop them from getting here.

By the sound of the explosion, I knew it was one of our mines that had scattered Simon to the winds. He had made a break for it across one of our flanks where a combination of our side's mines had mixed with theirs. Behind us, for about five miles, the Church of the Nativity was surrounded by thousands of our own hidden explosives. I don't think you could move one metre without encountering one. Though on second thoughts, the number of our own soldiers that had removed them with their lives had made little pockets of less danger.

The enemy mines are buried to our forward line. We watched them plant them. It was mid-morning when the sky went black with drones sweeping in. We managed to take a few, there were so many it was hard to miss. Ultimately it was another useless effort. Like swatting bees with a newspaper in the middle of a swarm.

This had the effect of cutting off all the trenches from the rest of the world. The manned outposts dug into the land, had been placed to create two tactical fronts. Firstly, it meant that every angle of attack on the ground was covered. Each post was positioned to cover the maximum land with the minimum of troops. They were far enough apart to not be able to shoot each other by accident and close enough to ensure a bullet was capable of reaching any part of the land being covered.

The second tactic was to create a false corridor to try and tempt the invaders to attack. Should they try to get through the gaps, the crossfire from us on the ground, plus the mines and the firepower bedded in behind us, would be so intense that the invaders would sustain many casualties.

The problems with these tactics had been that the enemy hadn't played along. They have kept their distance, blocked us in with their own mines and bombarded us with long-range energy weapons. We haven't seen a single foot soldier, tank or aircraft. Just a constant barrage of fire with no way out. I swear, apart from the third day, more of our troops have been killed just trying to get out of here than by any direct hit.

Now only six of us were left at the 'Spider Link Five Seven Outpost'. Six from an original attachment of one hundred and fifty men and women. All trained in double quick time to face an enemy that our commanding officers knew very little about. One hundred and fifty souls sold on the idea of freedom and liberty. Our entire race, our entire world was being threatened and they needed a bigger army quickly. One hundred and fifty young and enthusiastic fighters, reduced to just twenty-seven between 8:15 am and 10:26 am on the third day of being in the outpost.

That was the day they arrived.

We would have called for reinforcements but all our radio equipment was knocked out in the attack. The powers that be didn't seem to care, otherwise they would have sent more troops when they realised we couldn't be contacted. Or maybe they thought we had lost the fight and just decided that more troops would be wasteful. Maybe they had been wiped out.

*****

The distant sounds of heavy artillery started again followed seconds later by the explosions of the shells making contact with the ground. Here we go again. I sometimes think of what life would have been like if we weren't at war. I was sixteen when I was drafted. I didn't mind, it seemed like a laugh and I was doing my bit to help rid the world of this evil, protect my family and get the chance to be a hero instead of the layabout I was bound to become. I was eighteen when I was deployed to these trenches six months ago. I'm nineteen now.

The lads tried their best to celebrate my birthday, we'd been reduced to thirty by then so it wasn't a bad bash. In a twisted way, I felt as if all the mushroomed flames of the falling shells were some kind of fireworks display. It helped for a moment, but the next day we all felt the same crash of reality. Back to shooting at nothing and watching others die, each of us wondering when it would be our turn.

Sometimes I forget who we're fighting, and why. Christ, there's only six of us left. This is madness, I've got to get out. Get out. GOTTA GET OUT!

Hang on I've got to get a grip. That's what happened to Simon. He counted how many were left then made a run for it. Though in a way I think he is better off now.

Six privates against an army of relentless killing machines hell-bent on wiping humanity from the face of the Earth. Yeah, he's better off. I wonder who'll be next?

Steve has always been the strongest of us. When the captain bought it, he was the one who took charge. We had three sergeants and six corporals, but it was Steve who seemed to have his wits about him. I think he'll end up here on his own and when the war machine comes in to take their prize he'll be here yelling abuse at them.

Ian, on the other hand, amazes me that he's still alive. From day one he was always throwing out negative comments. I thought he'd be the first one killed, by our troops. Now he sits silently most of the time. He only screams out the word why, every so often in the midst of the shelling.

Dave always has a joke to tell, usually bad ones but I'll give him credit, when it comes to trying to keep the spirits up, he does his best. I don't know how he manages to keep such a positive note on things. He knows as well as the rest of us that we're going to die here yet he still carries on smiling and joking.

Chris keeps himself to himself. He'll join in with the conversations but doesn't give anything away. He says the less we know about him the less we can say if captured. Though being captured is a hopeful thought. I think he loves this, like he was born for it. He's the only one that still fires the bombs off.

Sammy I think will be the next to try and run, he has that look in his eye, the one that says "I'd rather die trying to get out of here than die just sitting on my arse." I give him two days before he goes for it.

Then there's me, a layabout teenager turned into a man by the army. Sold on the idea of freedom and righteousness, and now I sit watching the fields, listening to the bombs. This is my lot and this is where it will end, I kissed the book, took the shilling and packed a bag for my place in history. I only hope that something will be learned from this and in the future others won't have to endure this lonely life of getting used to death.

"Fuck ton of death."
(reprise)

The sharp piercing crack of Ms Nikita slapping her hands together in applause caused Duncan the same discomfort as the imp which counted the seconds with a snare. The producer had the widest smile that her porcelain face could muster before distorting into mania. She looked over at her lawyer and laughed. A full-hearted laugh that expresses joy and relief. Then she stopped clapping but continued to laugh while wagging her finger at the writer.

"I knew you had it in there." She stood up and walked around the table, "I knew you had all that death and torment tucked away in that little ol' head of yours."

Duncan felt his body relax. All the fear he had previously tried to repress had flowed out through the joy of hearing Ms Nikita's loud approval. From being so confident that he was, for once, ahead of the game, to being so terrified he thought she might actually kill him because he hadn't written something she liked. This had been both the worst and best meeting in this office.

"Thank you." He breathed deeply. "I must admit I wasn't that confident with this one, I'm so pleased you like it. Well, relieved more's the point."

Ms Nikita again stood behind Duncan, hands on his shoulders. Again, she dug her thumbs into his muscles as she spoke, only this time it was more pleasurable.

"You are one of those writers *my pretty*, that just needs a little *motivation* every now and then."

"I know, that's why I love having you on my side. You know how to get the best out of me."

"And I must say," she moved her hand to each side of

his head, "I got the best out of you at last."

With a swift twist, Duncan's neck made the sound of a sealed bottle of pop being opened, just without the hiss. The writer slumped in his seat and Ms Nikita placed his head at such an angle it was obvious this was not a man trying to get some sleep. She produced a small bottle of hand sanitiser from her jacket pocket. The lawyer sat dispassionate, as he watched his client go through the motions of ensuring every part of her hands were clean.

"I trust, Mr Chamberson, your company can make this look like an Epstein?"

"I'll get the team on it right away, Ms Nikita." He stood up and walked over to the phone on his desk. "We'll add it to your bill."

"Thank you, Mr Chamberson."

The lawyer ordered the cleaning service and then replaced the phone in its cradle. "May I speak candidly Ms?"

"Go right ahead."

"Won't staging this suicide, with all that unsavoury pornography and the newspaper leak, harm Mr Brashill's reputation and also the success of that story."

"Oh no, Mr Chamberson." She picked up Duncan's document case. "That little ol' war story is just perfect for Steven Steiner's next writer, director project."

"I'll get the contracts drawn up now."

"Oh, and that space story, I think Ridley's into that sort of thing. Maybe put Jon's name on it?"

"It's about the dangers of social networks."

C. J. Davies

In the city of Tokyo, almost twenty-three thousand square kilometres of concrete is playing home to nearly fourteen million people. Seas of neon lap the shores of traditional architecture in a melting pot of culture that has a flavour all of its very own. From lavish restaurants to bars where you can be served your drinks by young girls dressed as cats. This is the place to indulge your creative demon.

So many bars blend into one that, should you wish, Tokyo can be the perfect place to disappear. The Western Star is a small drinking establishment with an adequate jazz pianist, very few patrons and highly dangerous credit terms on the bar tab. It was bought by the Yakuza as a front for running their various schemes; hence the lack of regulars. They leave it open in order to get a drink anytime they wish, and for those that know how to stay silent, it is the perfect place to become one with alcohol without being seen.

Sitting in the shadows away from the entrance Bertie Fisher is making the finishing touches to his latest work. He has lived long enough to know the old days were as shit as the modern ones. Only now we have *social networks* and *video platforms.* It's not that he despises all things new, just the people that use those new things. His disdain for people has driven him here. Now he can work in a bar with the right customer to alcohol ratio.

He takes a large gulp to empty his glass of fine Japanese gin. Through the bottom of his glass he sees a silhouette, the outline of a woman that even through his low-resolution booze blurred sight, he recognised. That red jacket, those flowing chiffon trousers. By the time he placed the glass back on the table, Ms Nikita was standing right in front of him offering a fresh mother's ruin, and holding a large bourbon for her.

"Howdy, Bertie."

"Ah, Ms Nikita. However did you find me?" He raises his index finger to his lips. "Shhhh, don't tell me. It might fuck with my mind."

She takes a seat at his table and smiles. Bertie has always been one of her favourites. He never gets in any trouble, always delivers and never asks for anything more than what was first agreed. He is the troubled soul that produces great art. It was enough for him to have good food, a bed and an outlet for his words. He lived free of the trappings of modern life and yet stayed a slave to his creative tormentor, his need to write.

"I swear you are getting harder to find."

Bertie smiled, "What can I say? I like to make it hard for you. Anyway, how did you know I'd finished."

"I always know when you have finished Bertie." She places her hand in Bertie's and rubs it gently. "We have a contract, remember?"

Ms Nikita knows that Bertie likes to play this little game of tease. The touch of the hand was the sum amount of physical contact he has with another. It was something that Bertie appreciated.

He nods at Ms Nikita as a silent *thank you.*

"Now, enough of this foreplay," she says before exaggerating her accent. "Read me the god-damn story!"

28 days of Social Posts
By
Bertie Fisher

Day 1

I have been challenged. Though it was not today that this gauntlet was drawn across my face and tossed down at my feet. It was some months ago that this strangest of games, without rhyme or reason, was posted to me via the messenger app as part of Facenet. The task does not seem an arduous one. Simply, it has been requested of me by a 'friend' that I have never met, to keep a day-by-day account of all that I see, hear and do for the next 28 days.

The rules are very simple. Each morning I shall rise and, before dressing myself or commencing with any other morning routine, bar the evacuation of one's bladder, I must stand naked in front of the mirror and draw an invisible pentagram on my chest with the index finger of my left hand. Not just the star, but also the circle around it, drawn so that the edge touches each of the five points. This must be done while staring myself square in the eye and repeating seven times, "Doen wat verkeerd is in u hart."

What this is supposed to achieve I have no idea. As this is my first day I have very little to report. Simply breakfast, clothing and work. Maybe some magical forces will show themselves to me later, or maybe I'll get lucky and receive an email from some well-to-do Nigerian chap wanting me to help him move some money.

I have no idea why I am doing this ridiculous thing. I could have easily been posting up ten books in ten days that mean something to me, or listing ten albums or ten movies. Admittedly, all of these are just as pointless. However, there is something about this one that is telling me to give it a go. Maybe it's because I feel I'm not giving away any information about my bank account or my voting intentions? Maybe it's because I haven't seen anyone else doing it? Maybe I'm just bored and the devil makes work for idle hands? Whatever it is that's piqued my interest, at the very least, I can prove the falseness of this hokum.

Day 2

I don't know if it was the weather smashing itself into my bedroom window and fighting its way across my roof; the rather large but ultimately satisfying glass of Jameson's I had while watching *Only Connect*, or one of the ingredients from my rather opulent toasted sandwich. However, something from last night was responsible for giving me a weird dream. The sort of dream that has a hold on you for most of the following morning and, I suspect, going on into this evening.

It wasn't scary, more unnerving. I was standing, naked but for my rather dull boxer shorts on the upper level of an empty multi-story car park. It was cold and the wind swirled around me like the chasing breeze of racing cars moving too fast to see. Echoing off in the distance on another floor came the sound of laughter. It was a deep, slow, deliberate laughter as if the audience was trying to tell you how unfunny your jokes are.

I woke with a feeling of dread and guilt. It took me a few moments to remember who I was and why I was, in fact, awake. I went to the bathroom to relieve my bladder of the night's filtration and stopped to look in the mirror. My eyes looked heavy with the unsettled night. I drew the pentagram on my chest and muttered the words as per the challenge, then returned to bed for an extra 30 minutes.

So far today I've felt like a stranger in my own life. Not too dissimilar to a Monday comedown after a full-on weekend bender. But it's Tuesday and I only had the one, albeit rather a large, whiskey. Maybe I have the beginnings of a cold?

Day 3

I woke this morning to the sounds of the wind trying to break into my house. I lay in bed gazing at the ceiling for a moment. The pattern of the wallpaper was looking less pronounced with the latest layer of paint applied not less than two weeks ago. Making my usual noise that has been added to my morning routine with age, I climbed out of bed and set about performing my new ritual. Urination, the challenge in the mirror, brush teeth, get dressed.

Listening to the local radio station while sitting in my kitchen for close to 40 minutes, the news cycles past with tales of political nonsense and storm damage. This passage of time included two cups of coffee, some toast with a thin spread of Marmite, and a little scrambling around to get my bag ready for work. A quick look at the clock gave me the information that it was time to leave. I silenced the radio, grabbed my coat, bag and keys then, after checking three times that the door was locked properly, left for work.

Everything was as it was on any other day apart from the wind. The roads had the same amount of traffic. The same people walked, though not as briskly, along the pavements. I often wondered where they were all going. Was it to work or to medical appointments? Had they spent the night killing people and were now just clearing their heads? Did they ever talk to anybody else? I was deep into one of these thoughts when a woman stepped out in front of my car.

She seemed to come from nowhere. I managed to brake before fully colliding with her. She turned towards me and slammed her hands down on my bonnet. Her expression turned from glum to manic laughter to screaming at the top of her lungs. It was a scream so intense, so high in pitch, it made me feel physically sick, at which point I woke in my bed and vomited onto my bedsheets and duvet. The clock told me I was already an hour late for work. This made it easy for me to phone in sick and not feel guilty about it. I got out of bed and went to the bathroom as I needed to urinate and clean myself up. But, before I got in the shower, I drew the pentagram and said the words. After all, I have accepted the challenge so I mean to finish it.

Day 4

This morning my head felt like I had been kicked around by a giant cyclops while I tried to tame a manticore with a stool made from papier-mâché and a whip made of liquorice. I felt a duty to drag myself into work being as I had let everyone down yesterday. Even though I really didn't feel like it, I completed the challenge. My skin was sore and I could feel the pentagram this time as I drew it.

Work passed by as if it was a really dull T.V. programme playing in the background. Every so often I would notice a character I recognised, before realising I didn't care about them at all. Equally, I couldn't be arsed to reach for the remote and turn it over. I just wasn't quite me. The hangover from my sudden illness lasted all day affecting my general mood.

The drive home was uneventful. As I parked up I noticed a larger than normal charm of magpies had congregated on my front lawn. It might have been the general melancholy from my illness or the sudden silence of the corvids as I approached my gate. Whatever it was it made me feel quite uneasy as I walked past this Hitchcockian scene.

The house felt very quiet tonight, though at no point did I feel alone.

Day 5

The curious thing about doing a challenge is the compulsion it generates. Today is the fifth time I have stood naked in front of my full-length mirror in the bathroom drawing an invisible five-pointed star on my chest. The celestial icon edged off with a circle to make it seem more like the insignia of some Satanic cult. To say I am becoming bored with it is an understatement. However, even though I said to myself as I stared deep into my own eyes, "This is stupid. I'm not doing it," I suddenly noticed I was already halfway through the ritual.

My hand was quite out of my control as I watched it draw. It was like being entertained by an automaton with a sign that read: drop in a penny and see the naked man draw. Only, the mystic in the cabinet looked just like me doing this pre-programmed routine. Before I could even try to stop myself, I had uttered the words, "Doen wat verkeerd is in u hart." Each time I was thinking, "No more," before saying it again and again until all seven iterations were recited.

It has only been five days and already my mind has fallen into the repetitive cycle. I know I said I'd do this challenge. I know I said I always mean to finish what I start. But this challenge, this game, it...

Please excuse me. I'm just being silly. Still feeling like the tongue of a methylated spirits drinker. Once I get over this period of feeling utterly sorry for myself I can get back to being the life and soul of the online party; playing daft games and sharing memes about cats and going to the gym. I'll stop the challenge tomorrow, then start again when my head is in a much better place.

Day 6

Have you ever had the feeling you were in complete control, that nothing or no one could stop you? You just feel like the greatest thing in the universe. That was me this morning. For the first time in nearly a week, I felt great. My mind was sharp and focused, I was full of positive energy and ready to take on the world. I had been sat in work for just over an hour now and it has suddenly dawned on me. Despite my protestations, contrary to all my bravado about getting my head straight again, despite telling myself, "NO!" I still did the challenge this morning.

I genuinely thought I hadn't. If you asked me 30 minutes ago, "Have you done the 28-day pentagram bollocks this morning?" I'd have said, "No." I would have told you about shaving, brushing my teeth and wearing brand new never worn before boxer shorts. I would have provided you with a detailed account of my breakfast, which radio station I listened to on my way to work, and how annoying the traffic was. I would have told you I had stopped that stupid challenge. The fact is though, I did do it.

As I sit here at my desk I can feel it. Like a warmth digging into me. At first, I thought it was heartburn. I did have honey on toast this morning and that can at times give me a case of fire burps. Then I placed my hand over the warm patch. I traced my finger around the areas affected. It was as I drew the circle I realised what it was. That's when I remembered. After the toilet but before the shave. My new glorious outlook came crashing down. What on earth is wrong with me?

Day 7

OK, so I can't stop myself playing the bloody game/challenge thing. That seems obvious to me now. Even though it's my day off and I didn't get up at my usual time of 6:30 am, choosing to stay in bed until 10 am, I still drew the pentagram and said the words before anything else without a thought. It was just pure reaction. So, I have decided not to fight it. I'm going to let it happen.

My mind obviously wants this. It wants me to go through this imbecilic nonsense so I shall let it. Anyway, it's not like it's doing me any harm. In fact, I'm starting to feel quite good about things. My vision seems slightly improved and, now I'm clear of that daft lurgy, I feel dare I say, quite powerful. I'm not saying the challenge is what's having that effect on me. That would be grounds for a committal. This is me getting back on top and I'm just enjoying the ride and taking advantage of this positive wave.

So, I might not be in complete control, but I do feel good. I'll let this OCD thing ride its course. I'm sure it will stop itself after the 28 days are up. My mind will probably know that is the end of the challenge and it's time to stop. It is curious though how I can feel it. More than yesterday. Today I can feel the shape as warmth on my skin. It really is amazing what tricks the mind is capable of playing.

Day 8

I swear I'm not being paranoid. The day started off by waking up covered in sweat and screaming at the top of my voice. The neighbours must have thought someone was trying to kill me. The really strange thing is, despite being so terrified that my heart rate spiked and caused me to perspire like an overweight entertainer from the 1970s in an all-girl

Catholic school, I cannot remember a thing about it. Just the smell. A mixture of sulphur and bacon.

Once I sorted myself out, completed the morning challenge and ate breakfast, I drove to work. The unease I felt from the dream was all around me. Every person walking the streets was glancing at me with a knowing look. The shop assistant at the Tesco Express; the lollipop lady at the school crossing; even the old man sitting on the bench feeding the pigeons in the little park I pass en-route gave me a knowing, judgemental glare. I knew it was just in my mind, a hangover from the nightmare. But I also knew that they knew, they know, they…

They can see that something has changed, but unlike me, they know what it is. They can see what's different and it offends them. The lady that delivers the milk on the estate where I work was nearly physically sick at the sight of me. Though she did a great job of hiding it. But I could see her retching inside. The day cannot end quickly enough. I just need to get behind my closed doors and draw those curtains. Cut myself off from the world so they can stop thinking about me and the ugly I am today.

Day 9

I was disturbed from my slumber by a scratching noise. I opened my eyes to the darkness of the room. With no real focus to my eyes, and that persistent sound getting louder, it was hard to establish how long I'd been asleep. I called out "Alexa, what time is it?" to which the soothing voice of my Amazon bugging device replied, "The time is five seventeen ay em." I only had an hour left of my usual sleep, so I decided to get up.

The scratching had become more like someone

sawing in the corner of my room. Ignoring it for the moment I went to brighten my eyes and remove the fog from my mind, and urine from my bladder. I then completed the challenge at the double, before I returned to my bedroom to investigate.

For some reason, the use of a torch seemed a better option, rather than turning on the main light. Whatever was making that noise, I believed I had a better chance of finding it with the added focus of a limited area of illumination. There was no rhythm to the sound, just random bursts of grating harsh scrapes, as though someone had been buried alive in a gravel pit and was now digging their way out.

Controlling my urge to just rip everything apart I slowly and methodically set about moving objects to locate the source of my irritation. My glasses improved my vision and I could now read the display of my Echo clock. From getting out of bed, peeing, drawing symbols and reciting odd-sounding phrases to locating my tormentor, took a little over 30 minutes. In the corner of the left-hand window of my bedroom, I found a fly, cleaning itself.

I know it sounds crazy but that action of the fly using its front two legs to clean its eyes was as audible to me at that time of the morning as the workmen next door swearing at their tools in the mid-afternoon. I sat for a further 10 minutes just watching and listening to the bluebottle go though its very extended hygiene routine. Though, now I knew what it was, each scratch and scrape was more interesting than irritating. Then as suddenly as the sound was to wake me up, it stopped. The house felt very empty for a moment as silence flooded through the rooms, and for the briefest of seconds, and for the first time since I was a child, I was frightened.

Day 10

Today I was at the gym. I don't do the weights. The idea of hanging about in a room of heavy things while listening to other much stronger men grunt and moan while lifting said heavy things leaves me feeling sick and inadequate. Like being back at university listening to the alpha male in the next room loudly conquer his latest willing twink bottom. Banging the bed against the wall and making guttural noises of an ever-increasing volume until one final declaration of pleasure, then relief. As silence fell I usually had about 20 minutes to get my work done before they started up again. I do not wish to experience such a thing again by either living next door to a passionate couple nor by way of having that memory provoked by burly men trying to increase their burliness.

I go to swim up and down in a regimented way. Into the pool, 50 lengths and out. No hanging about in the changing rooms. No chitter-chatter with the other males. No eyeing up the female swimmers. Get the job done as fast as possible and leave. There is however the odd occasion where I stop on my way to the pool and look at myself in the mirror. Against these other specimens of masculine evolution, I am somewhat out of shape. I don't notice my belly at home, but here I stand out like a fat man at the gym.

Today however I noticed I seem to be losing some bulk. My profile didn't seem as vile and my swimming shorts felt a little loser. Maybe after five years of swimming three times a week, it's finally starting to have an effect. I also thought, which was the reason for stopping in front of the mirror, that I could see a darkening of the skin on my chest. Like a bit of a suntan only I do not bare my flesh to Magec's smile, ever. The last time this chest saw the sun was at the local lido when I was about eight years old. Secondly, the browning was in the shape of the pentagram I have been drawing each morning. Though it must have only been a trick of the light because as soon as I walked closer to my reflection for a better look, it was gone.

Day 11

Coincidence can really mess with your mind. Today the weirdest thing happened and now I'm still thinking about it, trying to rationalise it. I am a man of science. No hang on I'm not a scientist. What I mean is I am not a man of fantasy. Though I do like a good book or film completely based on fiction. How do I explain this? I like to think I have a good grip on what is real and plausible as opposed to that which is folk tales and fairy stories.

Today, when I was at the Tesco Express buying my £3 meal deal lunch of a cheese and pickle sandwich, Innocent Berry smoothie and a packet of Flaming Hot Walkers crisps, a man decided to get all arsey with me. All I did was ask him if I could get through to the drinks. He turned with such a look of aggression I was taken aback. He spat out his short response of, "What!?" before moving forward and getting right in my face. I have never been able to fight and felt quite intimidated by this bully who seemed hell-bent on turning this into a violent incident. That's when I said it.

It's quite unlike me to return any sort of vocal response in such an altercation other than a shame-filled "sorry," before hiding somewhere else. I do this even if it means I don't get what I want. But for some reason, some inexplicable reason, I narrowed my eyes and hissed in a low whisper, "I hope you fucking die."

He punched me and I fell back into a stacked trolley

of biscuits waiting to be put on the shelves. The shop staff were fantastic and managed to intervene before he did any more damage. Even though the man didn't leave quietly, making sure everyone in the store had a sample of how many swear words he knew, there was no more violence toward me or any other person.

About a minute or so after he had left, while the staff and other shoppers were still checking I was OK, there was a thud followed by the sound of screeching tyres. We all ran out to see what had happened. A light blue BMW was stationary in the road outside the shop. The smell of rubber hung in the air and the driver was getting out and moving quickly to the front of his car. He stopped and held his head in shock. Lying on the floor, wedged under the car was the man who had attacked me.

From what the witnesses were saying, and just looking at the scene, I figured he had tripped at the side of the road and fallen in front of the car. His head had collided with the front of the bonnet taking the full force of the vehicle before the driver had time to brake. This had the effect of pushing him, face first, into the road before his arms and torso became crushed by the wheels. The road was a pool of blood and it was quite obvious he had not survived the accident.

Realising this made me feel sick, especially after what I had said to him. Then I entertained the notion that I caused this, that I had willed it. Maybe it's the challenge? Drawing a demonic symbol on myself every morning without even thinking about it may have made me imagine I had such powers. Maybe it was the chemicals still flowing through my brain after the excitement of the confrontation that made me feel pleased, then guilty about what had occurred? And then, maybe it's just one of a billion random events that happen every day? A coincidence. Maybe?

Day 12

I decided to go to the library. I must admit that I'm not a frequent visitor. I think the last time I sat silently amongst these books must have been nearly five years back. I was doing research into the history of a local business. I have found that if you go into a family-run establishment forearmed with knowledge of their history their defences drop and it becomes easier to sell advertising to them. I am no longer in that job, and as such have had little reason to visit these bookshelves.

My intention was to find books about the paranormal. Not the popular section filled with fake psychics pedalling their lies. I wanted the old dusty unread tomes filled with the learning of those that believed in all this pentagram stuff. Granted, it was a long shot and I was basing this idea on what I'd seen in films and read in books over the years. I imagined a room in the back of the library. Shelves of accent leather-bound books filled with hard to read typefaces. The sort of place you needed to wear white cotton gloves just to touch the publications.

My local library does have a number of old books about the dark arts and the room they were in was indeed old, as in the 1980s old. Instead of dusty old books, they were on microfiche. And instead of an old man who looked like he had lived for at least a couple of centuries, I was reminded how to use this antiquated equipment by a very charming woman in her 30s.

With no real idea where to start, I thought I'd look for references to the pentagram. I wasn't sure what I was looking for, I only knew that something felt different. Like the events of the previous day had changed something in me. Paranoia was creeping in and I guess I just wanted to prove to myself that all these spooks and spectre thoughts floating around in my head were complete and utter nonsense. And for a good hour and a half, it was.

Then I found a small article in a kid's book called Earth Magic for Children written by Edith Elv in 1878. Most of the book consists of stories of Old Nick living under a bridge at the back of the garden or how Satan 'the ultimate trickster' would entice children away from their parents. Typically, these were tales designed to scare kids into behaving. However, towards the back of the book, there was a section called 'How to raise the Devil' which gave detailed instructions on how to allow Beelzebub to come forth and walk on the earth.

It described how each morning you should stand in front of a mirror and draw a pentagram on your chest while saying "Do what's wrong in your heart." It even had a pictogram showing you how to draw the symbol. The only thing different from what I was doing was the words. Mine sounded foreign or made up. Maybe it was a translation.

I felt sick and had to get out. I thanked the lady and left in a hurry making far too much noise as I did. As I hit the air my stomach contracted and breakfast fell onto the pavement.

This must have been where they got it from, whoever that friend was.

I took out my phone and fired up my messenger app. I don't interact that much so finding the challenge message was easy. A cold flow of horror chilled my blood as I read the name of the person who sent me the challenge: Edith Elv.

Day 13

A quick internet search revealed nothing about this Edith Elv. I could find no record of her on-line at all. Her book 'Earth Magic for Children' appears on none of the lists I could find. Not even in the rare, out of print catalogues. I'd almost given up hope when, by chance, I happened upon a person with the same surname on one of the social networks. A quick scan of their wall led me to a post they shared about two years ago. It claimed that they had traced their family tree back to an author called Edith (1805-1879) and that she was into witchcraft. There were many comments from friends saying this modern Elv had obviously taken after the family witch, followed by others declaring the comments to be 'lol'.

There was a link to the family tree website they had used. Clicking this proved illuminating. At the top of the screen, there was a graphical representation of a family tree consisting of something that looked like a squashed oak with the wrong shaped leaves. Under this was the name Edith Elv with all the information about where she was born; where she got married; and where she was living during the mandatory censuses.

Now I knew where Edith had come from.

Maybe a little trip to West Sussex would prove fruitful? Reading the name of the town certainly made me feel like going. As if it was drawing me to it. As if it was calling me, so to speak.

I rang my boss, arranged the week off and booked the train tickets for tonight. I then booked a small, cheap B&B in Worthing, not too far from Clapham village. This is where the only Edith Elv I can find anything about, was born. She lived here all her life as far as I could tell. She married, but unusually for the time, she kept her maiden name. Her three children, Nicolas, Gabriel and Emma all took on her name instead of their father's and that whole branch of the family tree where Elvs instead of Coopers. Maybe I will find something to answer these questions I have in my head? If not, maybe the breakaway will just do me some good?

Day 14

I arrived at the Hecate B&B in Worthing just before dinner. The train journey down was dull. The rhythmic *clickety-clack* of the track combined with the unnatural warmth of the carriage caused me to frequently nod off, which helped pass the time. But for the strange dreams of a golden retriever giving sermons about the need to be one with nature before sacrificing an albino pug in a rather gruesome way, the journey would have been very pleasant.

The landlady is Charlie Stride: mid-to-late 50s and still thinking she has what it takes to capture any man or woman she desires. Time hasn't been kind to her, but then again, she does seem to have some kind of aura that is enticing. She gave me my room key and, even though I only paid for bed and breakfast, she insisted on making me some dinner.

The decor in this place is dated. Browns and dark oranges. Geometric shapes in the wallpaper and highly patterned carpets. It was like stepping back into my childhood. Pictures of fantasy images hung on the walls. Dark wooden frames encasing pictures of tree monsters, fairies, elves, and witches. Even the way Ms Stride was dressed in a flowing pale blue loose-fitting outfit, tie-dyed with purple at the cuffs, sleeves and hem of the dress, felt very Wiccan. Drawing a pentagram on myself in the morning would feel quite normal here.

The food was lovely. A mushroom stew with potatoes

and a sourdough bread. She even furnished me with a glass of red wine. Not my normal tipple, but it would have been rude to turn her down. The journey was catching up with me and all I wanted to do was lie down and rest, start my search in the morning. I bid Ms Stride a goodnight and retired to my room.

Day 15

Last night I dreamt of walking in the woods. As I strode forward the foliage that had overgrown and covered the well-trodden path receded back to the fringe of the trail. Everywhere I looked, in the bushes, behind the trees, rushing through the undergrowth there were dogs. Black, brown, white, big, and small. There were dogs everywhere, just out of sight. I knew they were there. I could hear them, growling and whining and panting. I just could never get a clear look at one. No matter how hard I tried, every time I turned, they just nipped in behind something.

The bed felt very comfortable as I woke up. I knew I didn't want to go back to sleep but it had been so long since I felt this relaxed. I dragged myself up and enacted the usual routine of toilet, draw, chant, wash. The challenge didn't feel stupid, or a chore. I left my room and went down for breakfast. Ms Stride had prepared a lovely plate of toasted sourdough with smashed avocado drizzled with sesame seed oil. Normally I would just declare this to be some sort of hipster crap trendy bollocks, but it looked so nice. Her voice had enough energy to fill me with the enthusiasm to eat any food.

"The Devil will grab your tail," my host declared as she put the plate down in front of me, "if you are too fat to run." Then she laughed a genuine giggle before she returned to the kitchen .

I sat alone and ate my food. It was so much nicer than I would have ever imagined. I straightened my spent breakfast wares and left the dining room. In the hall/reception area there was a poster on the wall near a payphone for a local taxi firm WARTAX. I programmed the number into my mobile and then called it.

Clapham village lies about six miles to the northwest of Worthing, about a 20-minute taxi ride. The driver was friendly enough. He insisted on giving me a local history lesson as we wound our way through the suburban streets and out onto the country roads. I was trying not to listen, being fully focused on locating my mysterious author. That was until he started talking about the Clapham Woods. I didn't want to ask him to repeat himself so I made a mental note to research 'the devil and Satan worship rituals,' as my driver put it, after today's little trip.

Clapham village was as picturesque as you would expect. Postcard-perfect houses crowned with thatched roofs and a quaint parish church made of local flint. The graveyard surrounding the religious building was old but well kept. I felt the church was as good a place as any to start. The sun was out with a light breeze keeping the air very cool.

I strolled up to the church and entered its ground via the lychgate. As I stepped through, the breeze dropped and the warmth of the sun broke through. It would have been easy to believe this had just turned into a summer's day rather than being the back end of winter bordering spring. I meandered between the gravestones reading names and dates as I strolled. All the graves were old. The newest I saw was 1922, and that marked the last resting place of Mary Longfellow who lived to the ripe old age of 98, which would be impressive for nowadays, let-alone back then.

Then I saw it: the small, unassuming stone of Edith Elv. Most of the engraving had worn away with the years but her name was still easy to read. I wasn't sure how I would feel if I found it. Excitement or fear or dread or...

I don't know.

I did know it wasn't how I felt when I found the grave. I wasn't expecting to feel so calm. I had a sudden sense of déjà vu and the breeze picked up again, which made me shiver. I knew this was where I needed to be. Quickly I headed back into the village to see if I could book a room.

After booking a night's stay at the Old Dairy I called a cab back to my digs in Worthing so I could pick up a few bits and explain to Ms Stride that I wouldn't be back tonight. She was great and told me the people of Clapham are, "Just wonderful earthy people." She also told me if I wanted a drink I would have to go to the neighbouring village of Patching where the Wicca's Basket serves a nice pint and quality food. I might eat there tonight and see if I can meet some of the locals.

Day 16

Last night I went to the 'Wicca's Basket'. My plan was to have a couple of pints of the local brew, a good bit of pub grub and to try to get a feel for the place. The owner of the Old Dairy, where I had rented a room for the night, asked me what my plans were for the evening. When I told him what my intention was he kindly offered me a lift. It turns out it's his local watering hole and he explained that the local police seemed to be somewhat creative towards the single road the villagers drive up and down of an evening, and the implementation of current drink driving laws. A couple of weeks back I would have been appalled to hear such a blatant disregard for the law. However, something about this country air seems to have softened my view and now it doesn't seem that big a deal.

We arrived just after 8:00 pm. The place was packed. One would have thought that the residents of at least three villages were in attendance tonight. Mark, my host and driver noticed a couple of spare seats at a table. To me, the two women in their mid-40s already had a claim to the table. One was wearing a pale blue 1950s style dress with white polka dots. The other was wearing a deep orange loose-fitting blouse. As we got closer I could see she was also wearing dark blue tight-fitting jeans. I think Mark either knew or was known by every person in the pub. We arrived at the seats and Mark introduced me to the two women. Joan in the blue dress and Kate in the tight jeans.

We sat down and Mark went to buy drinks, including the ladies in the round. I engaged in a little small talk. Kate seemed to have a similar awkwardness to myself, Joan, on the other hand, was full of chatter. Mark returned with his catch and asked if I wanted food. I just said, "Some random pie and chips," to which Mark then refused my money before going to order it. Joan found my response rather amusing and I felt I was warming to her.

The night continued for another couple of pints before things took a turn. I remember saying I felt dizzy. I remember everyone in the pub laughing. At some point, I was sitting on a chair being lifted above the crowd. People were shaking my hand, maybe even kissing my hand.

Some of these images felt like memories while other glimpses feel like a dream. I'm sure I wouldn't have been shirtless in the middle of a public house with Kate fellating me while an old man cut the throat of a bichon frise before pouring its blood all over my chest. Letting the red warm sticky liquid drip onto Kate's face and hair.

There were faint images of staggering through the middle of an orgy still covered in the blood of that small curly lap dog. The next thing I think I remember was lying naked on my bed at the Old Dairy. Above me was Joan, still wearing her blue dress with white polka dots. She had a leg on either side of my waist and my penis was fully inserted into her vagina. Her eyes were closed and she moaned as she moved her pelvis back and forth rubbing her clitoris against my pubis. The enjoyment she seemed to be experiencing had very little to do with me. She lifted her head up, and for a moment, as her face was illuminated by a shaft of moonlight breaking in through the curtains, I could have sworn she turned into Ms Stride from the Hecate B&B. I felt frightened and yet I couldn't speak or move.

As I opened my eyes to the sun invading my room via the same crack in the curtains that the moon had used, everything felt surreal. There was no sign that Joan or anyone else had been in my room. I was not covered in blood and my clothes were folded in the way only I fold my clothes. Now I am standing in front of the mirror. My general feeling is to do the challenge, throw up and return to bed until I can clear my head enough to make some sort of sense of it all.

Day 17

After returning to bed yesterday I slept straight through to this morning. Somehow I had not wet the bed but the relief I felt once I stood in front of the toilet and the urine began to flow was remarkably pleasurable. The pentagram on my chest felt warm which made it very easy to trace. The words fell out of my mouth as if I wasn't even saying them. I must have needed that sleep because I felt fantastic.

The images from the pub, or more, the feelings those memories gave me weighed heavy. My body felt powerful, my mind sharp. But the fog of shame and regret coupled with the uncertainty of whether it was real or just a dream gave the world an uneasy ambience. I skipped breakfast and avoided Mark. Even if only the chair dance was true, it was still embarrassing enough to make me want to hide. My intention was to return to the church and ask the vicar if he or she knew anything about the Elv's of Clapham.

The air was as still as the eye of a storm, though the sun's warmth was refused entry to the surface by the clouds. I entered the grounds through the lychgate and headed straight for Edith's headstone. The horror I found made me vomit on the spot.

Draped over the top of the author's stone was the disembowelled carcass of a bichon frise, though its fur was no longer white. The blood that was lost in its violent end stained the poor thing's soft curls. The dog's innards, hacked out by the brutal frenzy of a maniac with a butcher's knife, lay upon the ground around the foot of this humble monument. The top of the gravestone had been inserted into the cadaver via the large gaping hole left behind by the savage way in which the internal organs had been removed. It looked as if the creature had been impaled on the weather-smoothed stone.

Blood had soaked into the headstone causing the grey to darken. I felt weak at the knees but somehow managed to remain standing. My attention was taken so much by this celebration of cruelty and gore that when the reverend spoke in a surprisingly northern accent, she made my heart skip a beat.

"This is so awful," she said. "Just awful."

"Have you called the police?"

She looked at me like I had just told her I eat children. "Why?" she stepped over to the body of the dog and started to gently stroke its head, "When we did this for you?"

As if I had been struck by a lightning bolt my mind lit up. I remembered everything. The pub, the sacrifice, the orgy, slitting Joan's throat while Mark and Kate performed cunnilingus on her. The force of the blood hitting my face as she orgasmed. I remembered having sex with Ms Stride wearing Joan's blood-stained dress.

The world around me started to feel as if it was caving in. I fell to my knees. Power surged through my veins, but not something I could control. Then I smiled. It was at that moment I became aware of the others. Not sure how many, but enough to pick me up and carry me to the church.

Day 18 - 22

I am awake. The vicar puppeteered my hand to draw the pentagram on my chest while my mouth spat out the words as a reflex action. I was merely an observer. I recorded the passing of time by watching the colours being projected by the sun through the stained-glass window. The light moved slowly across the pews. I barely breathed. During these daylight hours, others came. Unlike the vicar they keep their faces covered. Each of them is turning up to worship me while I am bound naked to a chair. Each sick fuck wears the face of a mutilated dog.

They bring me food and drink. In front of my eyes, the vicar pours what looks like blood onto the offering before force-feeding me. I only struggled the first few times. After that, it started to taste quite nice. In fact, I started to crave it. The added iron-enriched drizzle took on a sweetness. With each mouthful, I felt stronger. My mind was still trying to catch up with events.

This was the routine for days. The colours would start on the western wall and move across to the east. Each day the dog people came. Their worship started to feel good. As they praised me, I could feel a power welling up deep inside. The vicar kept feeding me, and I barely breathed. But there was something about all this that felt temporary.

The fifth day passed and the colours of the stained-glass windows faded as darkness laid down upon the earth. The last of the dog people had left and the vicar was off to see them out. I got thinking about my bonds. I imagined the knots becoming loose and easy to untie. In my head I watched the rope move, like a snake, untangling itself from around my hands. I felt them slacken.

The vicar returned to give me more wine mixed with blood. As she raised the golden goblet to my mouth I reached up and grabbed her by the throat. Rising out of my seat I slowly lifted her off the ground, squeezing hard enough so she couldn't scream, but not so hard as to kill her or render her unconscious. I wanted to see the fear in her eyes. With my other hand, I took the drink and consumed it quickly, allowing some of the fluid to spill out of my mouth and onto my chest. I smiled at the vicar before throwing her into the pews. The speed of the impact smashed her through the wooden seating. She eventually stopped three rows from the back in a bloody, lifeless heap.

I walked over to the font by the south door and washed myself down. I could see from the steam rising out of the pool of warm blood that the air was cold, though I didn't feel it. I strolled back to the altar and dried off on the dossal. My clothes were neatly folded and stacked on a chair behind the pulpit. I dressed and, after taking one last look around, left via the main doors.

Day 23

I waited in the woodland surrounding the village of Clapham until first light. My need to complete the drawing of the pentagram and utter the chant was stronger than it had ever felt before. After I had done the ritual and made myself comfortable from bladder pressure I searched for a hiding place with an excellent view of the church.

Slightly in from the edge of the woods I came upon a mighty oak. Her branches were strong; her trunk thick with the many years she had stood guard over this place. She knew what I wanted and she was willing to help me. I scaled her ancient bark and positioned myself. The sun had moved into the sky when the first of the villagers came. It was Mark from the Old Dairy. He approached the lychgate, stopped to put on his mask made from the face of a German shepherd, then continued up to the main door.

I imagined him looking at the aftermath of violence with horror and completely missing the irony of the agony caused in the creation of his mask. I could feel his fear and rage. He was offended by my actions. I pictured him talking to himself and gave him the idea to gather everyone from the sect in the church as quickly as possible. The next thing I saw was Mark coming out into the graveyard to make phone calls. Within minutes every door in the village had opened and the occupants descended on the church. I could feel this wasn't all of them.

Within the hour some 15 cars had arrived. One was

driven by Ms Stride from the Hecate B&B. Another was Joan's friend Kate. They all made their way into the church. Now they were all arguing. Some were saying this was supposed to happen, others said that I should be grateful to them. I dropped down from the oak and slowly walked towards the church.

In my mind, I locked the doors.

I thought about ivy growing fast to cover the doors and windows before willing the plants to expel any fluids they held, instantly drying them to tinder. With the click of my fingers, I sparked a flame and told everything to burn hotter than the fires of hell.

Their screams were like music to me. I stood smiling, watching the fire jump up the walls, forcing its way into the roof space and burning the rafters. The stained-glass windows melted in the intense heat before the roof collapsed and silenced this evil congregation. As the fire raged, I walked through the lychgate and up to Edith's grave. I now knew who she was and I knew what she wanted. I removed the corpse of the dog and placed a hand on the blood-stained stone.

"Doen wat verkeerd is in u hart," I said as I drew a pentagram on the face on the gravestone. The shape ignited and burned within the lines of the pattern.

I walked back to Worthing, back to the Hecate B&B and retrieved my belongings. I never heard a single siren. I gathered my backpack, wrote "Thank you for a lovely time," in the visitor's book, then left. Time to return home.

Day 24

The train ride home last night was dull. The constant sound of the tracks grated on my frayed nerves, like the sound of someone rubbing blocks of polystyrene together while a small child, with no sense rhythm, bangs on a Tupperware box. I found amusement in making people do things. Nothing overtly nasty. Subtle little things like getting the burly gym type to spill his expensive water onto the crotch of his light grey jogging pants. Or draining the mobile phone battery of the young lady two seats down just to stop her playing that bloody candy game.

After more hours than I care to spend in the company of so many people that I can now smell, I arrived home. The house felt full of life. I could feel every fly, every spider. The mice under the floorboards in the kitchen; I could hear their hearts beating. The smell of the mould in the bathroom was not musty and damp but full of life. It had a reason for being there and was, like the rest of us, just trying to survive.

I sat in my front room listening to and feeling all these living creatures, plants and fungi. Each had its own motivations. All wanted the same thing: to live.

I felt connected to it all. This was my home, my environment. These life forms depended on me for survival and I needed them to keep each other in check. There was a whole ecosystem around me that I had never noticed nor even considered before.

I fell asleep and dreamed of open fires and pots of boiling blood and stewing bones. Waking up felt good, there are very few things better than waking in your own bed. The pentagram on my chest was now very visible and, as it had for a few days now, felt warm. Going down to the kitchen I realised it had been two whole days since I had eaten. I took everything I had in the freezer; some leftovers from about five weeks ago; a frozen pasta dish; a ready meal curry that had printed on the package that it contained chicken though on the many times I had sampled it I had questioned this claim. Everything; the oven chips; frozen vegetables; even the cheaters Yorkshire puddings.

I took it all and cooked it up.

All with pints of gravy.

I ate it slowly, savouring every mouthful and finishing one cobbled-together meal while another cooked in the oven. I kept eating and eating and eating until everything from the freezer was gone. I washed it all down with jugs full of cold water from the tap. After I had consumed the last of my cooking frenzy and had washed and put away the dishes, I retired to my front room where I sat, completely still, with no external stimuli. I sat as the sunset and the moon rose high above the horizon. I sat almost lifeless until the only light in the room came from the streetlights that tinted everything I owned with a piss-stain yellow.

At 10:00 pm I turned on the TV to watch the news. There was nothing about the fire I had started. I scanned the news sites on the web. Nothing. I dug deeper into the regional sub-pages for West Sussex and found nothing. I thought this was peculiar but, by the time it had taken to find nothing of real note, I felt sleep was needed.

Day 25

The pentagram on my chest is now very visible. Before, it was like a tan mark, slightly browner than the rest of my pale skin. Now, the pattern is black. Black and leathery, as if I had been branded. I can hear it crackle like frying bacon as I pull my finger over the lines. It has a slightly reddish glow, similar to charred embers when air is blown onto them in a dying fire, which appears briefly under my fingertip as I ritualistically trace the dark path. With each word of the incantation my heart slows. By the end of this day's ritual, challenge, addiction or whatever it is, I am hardly alive.

My breathing has become slow and shallow, my heart controlled. I hear everything. Conversation across the street, a couple in the house around the corner planning to murder an ex-lover; the weakening of the glass in my windows. I smell so much, the stench of a thousand bins waiting to be collected, it must be Tuesday. There is also the distinct aroma of guilt and shame oozing through the wall from next door as a wife cheats on her husband with his business partner. I hear her fake moans as her thoughts betray her. This is a punishment fuck to get at the husband for screwing some sales dolly at the Christmas party. The business partner is unaware of how much of a failure he is in bed. To him, she is very convincing.

I hear and smell and know all of this, and yet I still stand naked in front of the mirror. My belly has flattened and there is some muscle definition coming. Maybe even the beginnings of a six-pack. My penis seems less ugly to me. Everything about my body looks to have been corrected somehow. I feel no shame in being naked at all.

I know it's cold, I can see by the goosebumps on my arm that tell me the air is chilly, but I can't feel it. I feel neither hot nor cold. There is also no panic, no anxiety. I've been standing here for at least two hours now and I'm very late for work. But I don't care. The phone has rung twice in the last fifteen minutes. It's probably work trying to find out where I am, but I don't care.

I feel nothing.

My Echo clock turned on the radio as it should at 6:30 am. There has still yet to be any news on the fire down south. Maybe other events have bumped it out of the cycle. Maybe I just wished it to not be noticed. I cannot remember and I really don't care.

Day 26

It's time to return to work. I woke, jumped out of bed, ritual, wash, shave, breakfast and leave. The traffic was a lot lighter than I expected. It was only when I arrived at the office that I realised I was two hours early. It felt so odd because, even though it was dark, to me the world was bright. OK so the colours were not as I remember them being, but to not notice it was dark at all was something new.

A lot has changed in me since the Clapham village trip. I go between feeling amazing to being completely lost on an hour-to-hour basis. Today though, today I feel strong. My eyesight is better, my hearing is now like a superpower. This symbol on my chest feels like it is giving me energy as if I'm tapped into some cosmic generator that's taking its time to attune to me. AND I FEEL FUCKING GREAT!

Being early has its advantages. I get to see the dawn with these fresh eyes. The colours ripple in the sky like oil being trapped between two sheets of clear polyurethane then heated by a projector light, throwing the constant movement of the spectrum onto a wall. I can feel all the life, from the tiniest bug to the largest dog. Every plant, fungus, worm and bird; it was a cacophony of thoughts and impulses that were too loud to ignore. I also get to be here when Neil arrives.

Neil, the office pervert. Every woman in the place will not be left in a room with him on their own. The way he letched over Tina when she spent two weeks with us on work experience. She was fourteen. He was always parked up here before anyone else arrived. But not today. I heard his car coming from about a mile away. I sat in my car and waited.

His shiny white BMW pulled into the estate car park. My powers allowed me a glimpse of his thoughts, so I knew he hadn't seen me. He was having a fantasy about closing a deal with a female client then raping her on the desk. In his head, she was grateful and thanked him for not taking no as an answer. This piece of shit had to go.

I walked over to his car and stood by the driver's side. He looked up at me with a condescending smile. I pictured his heart in my hand and squeezed. The smile morphed into a grimace as he clutched his hands to his chest. With his lips turning blue, Neil started to have difficulty breathing. After a few short minutes, all of which he was in agony, he finally fell unconscious. I knew instantly he was dead. Even standing outside the car I could feel his life force just stop. I still gave it another ten minutes, just to be sure, then I phoned an ambulance.

The blue flashing lights painted the entire estate with their hue, casting shadows that seemed to dance. He was pronounced dead at the scene. Most of the staff were shocked but slightly pleased by the news. The one that surprised me was Wendy. Her thoughts betrayed a lusting for this vile human being.

I feel even more powerful now.

Today is going to be a good day.

Day 27

I had a dream last night that I was sitting on an onyx throne, around me the world burned and I laughed at its suffering. Every so often I would stand and shout out a reason I had done this then spit into the flames. "For the children, you abused," or, "For the greed in your pockets," or "For the lonely."

When my spittle hit the flames there would be an eruption of heat followed by the screams of a thousand bankers and politicians and business leaders as I immolated them. I was burning the flesh from their bones as an offering to those that had suffered by their hands. In amongst the flames, those that had been downtrodden and those that had been kept in servitude to the rich and powerful, all worshipped me. They are the meek and I have just unlocked their inheritance.

As I opened my eyes to the morning that was invading my room, I had a sense of achievement. My life now has a purpose. When I looked in the mirror and gave thanks for my power by way of the ritual and incantation, I stared deep into my own eyes. I didn't see me.

I saw something new.

I couldn't decide whether I was physically changing into a new person, a new being or just beginning to open my eyes and see reality for the first time since the day I was born.

My day at work was successful. People were still faux-mourning the loss of Neil. Some were milking it with great skill. They all stink to me. That repugnant stench of hypocrisy. These little people are as much a part of the problem as those that are keeping them in their holding-cells of aspiration. To them, money is love and perception is respect. To me, they are all just scavengers licking the boots of a master that sits back wanking while watching his servants fight for the leftovers with the hope that one day they'll be asked to sit at the table.

I talk on the phone to more people like these parasites. All out for themselves and no one else. I sell them stuff they don't need just to take their money. Right now I am beyond the height of any powers I used to have, selling to these weak-minded cretins is so easy. For a laugh, I convinced three of them to kill their pets. I know they will, I can feel them planning it already.

Any facade I used to put up just to exist in the office has gone. I laugh out loud when I think of something funny. I know what people think of me, I can hear their thoughts as if they were speaking. They know my name and that makes me happy. Maybe I will give them another couple of days working this millstone before I kill them all.

Day 28

The whites of my eyes are now a pale yellow, my irises, that once were blue, are now a dark deep burnt yellow and my pupils are more like black rectangular portraited slits than round portals to the soul. I know who I am. I know what I am. Most importantly I know why I am. For the first time in my life, I understand the reasons for everything. I know what I am here for.

As I draw my finger over the blackened flesh of the pentagram it ignites. I say the words, "Doen wat verkeerd is in u hart." I mix it with the English version, "Do what's wrong in your heart."

And I understand.

The only way to purge this earth is to scorch it. Burn everything, destroy it all. Take it to a point where all money is worthless and status means nothing. Take everything away so all that is left are a bunch of scared weeping childlike beings unable to fend for themselves. They will have to help each other to live.

Before, the idea of wiping out most of the human race would have been wrong in my heart. But I get it now. That is what I have to do. Do wrong in order to reset everything and make it alright again. The burning symbol on my chest had spread, now my whole front was ablaze, I could smell my flesh burning, hear it spitting and crackling and yet I could feel no pain.

I am still me, that is without a doubt. I have not been possessed by some spirit. I am just more than me, blessed with a strength of body and mind beyond anything I could ever have imagined. I have merged with forces so much greater than mere mortals. I live on a different plain now; I have a grander purpose. I am the harbinger of freedom. I am the saviour of all. I understand that everything you hold dear, what I used to hold dear, is nothing but sparkly dust created to divert our attention.

Well, I have been shown the truth; I can see the righteous path. As I stand here in front of my mirror, an inferno of boiling blood and charred meat I renounce the need for such material things like mobile phones, computers and televisions. I vomit on the need to sit in the window of social networks and voyeuristic platforms; craving to be seen by so many yet demanding privacy. As I step forward unto this world I will free its people from the tyranny of God and tear down the palaces of gold built in honour of wealth and power.

I am the reckoning. The end of now and the beginning of tomorrow. I am on my way.

Day 29

Profile deleted.

"It's about the dangers of social networks."
(reprise)

It happened so infrequently that Ms Nikita had almost forgotten what it felt like; the warm feeling inside her that signalled a positive emotion had just taken place. This was why she adored Bertie. His words always stirred something deep in her that no other writer could get close to. She had the ability to understand the others were good or at least marketable. But Bertie had a style that she really connected with. Bertie was more than just a client to her: she was a fan.

"I don't know how you do it."

Bertie finished his gin before putting the glass down a little heavier than he intended, "Yes you do."

Bertie had always known how Ms Nikita worked. Ever since that first meeting when she walked into the *Fork Me* cafe on the promenade of Blackpool seafront. The sound of the door opening made him look up from his fifty pence notepad which, along with his *Night of the Living Dead* t-shirt, wore the battle scars from his full English breakfast. That's when he saw her; as pale as a heroin addict with raven black hair and deep red lips, like a vampire after a feed. She was wearing clothes that looked like they cost more than the cafe.

It was uncanny how she picked him out of the other grease-infused patrons. Just walking straight over to him and sitting down opposite. He was impressed that she didn't wipe the seat first. He was also surprised that, looking the way she did, she wasn't sitting there with a look of disgust like some who had just stuck their finger through the toilet paper while wiping their arse. Little Miss Hollywood had walked into a greasy spoon and although she looked out of place, she seemed to fit right in.

They talked about his writing. She had read a couple of stories he'd sent to the American horror publication, *First Fright magazine*. She particularly liked the one about Devil worship.

"It was so refreshing to see *the goat* win in the end."

That's when she offered him a contract. That's when he knew. The fact she didn't want him to use his pen but a quill she had in her pocket. And the fact she claimed that ink was so overrated as she stabbed his thumb with the nib.

"We'll use blood ink."

All this evidence and yet, he didn't mind. Eyes wide open he signed knowing that whatever lay ahead of him was going to be better than this.

Sitting in a Yakuza run bar in Tokyo was perfect for him. To anyone in the outside world that managed to catch a glimpse, he appeared to be the definition of a man giving up on life. But the truth was: he was happy. It is the life that suits him. Permanently drunk in different bars around the world, never begging for money and being left alone to write his words. Only ever seeing the woman he loved for the briefest of times when he had completed his work. *Utter Bliss.*

"Tell me, Ms Nikita, what is it about this industry you love so much?"

"You know Bertie, in all the years I've been doing this, no one has ever asked me that before."

She pushes a fresh glass of gin across the table towards him. Bertie smiles as he never noticed her going to the bar. Her soft Kansas tone changes, still a southern belle, just less forced and more honest.

"All the people behind the scenes. The set builders, lights, sound, the people that make the clothes and the props.

All the talented people doing the makeup and the special effects. They are like the blood of the industry. Running around the veins and arteries making sure that everything works."

She points a finger at Bertie, her eyes betray an affection.

"Then there's you lot. The writers and the directors and the actors. Y'all like the beating heart. Pushing the blood around so that the monster has life."

"Does that make you the brain?"

Ms Nikita stands up, brushes herself down and prepares to leave. "No, Mr Fisher." Her professional tone returns. "I have its soul."

Printed in Great Britain
by Amazon

48923459R00118